C

Dex studied Wa...   ...ving.
The trapped man ga...   ...iery,
deep anger inside D...   ...had come during
boyhood, and which had never fully left him, even for a
moment, since.

"The devil take you," Murchison said again. Blood ran out
the corner of his mouth. "The devil take you to the hottest
pit of hell!"

Something inside Dex Otie seemed to break. Abruptly, he
cursed, drew his pistol again, and leveled it at Murchison. "If
I'm going to hell, you go first."

"If you've been pining for a writer to come along who brings
an inventive approach to a long-established literary genre,
Will Cade is your man. His is a fascinating new take on the
Old West, presented through fast-paced action, carefully
crafted plots, and a distinctively different and occasionally
quirky breed of characters. Will Cade is a creative new
writer you won't want to miss!"

—Cameron Judd, author of *Passage to Natchez*

FLEE THE DEVIL
WILL CADE

LEISURE BOOKS NEW YORK CITY

To Gus, always a loyal friend.

A LEISURE BOOK®

March 1998

Published by

Dorchester Publishing Co., Inc.
276 Fifth Avenue
New York, NY 10001

ISBN 0-8439-4367-X

The name "Leisure Books" and the stylized "L" with design are trademarks of Dorchester Publishing Co., Inc.

Printed in the United States of America.

FLEE THE
DEVIL

Part I
Death Train

Chapter One

Dexter and Canton Otie crested the hill at the same moment the railroad bridge a half-mile ahead of them gave way.

They yanked their horses to a halt and watched in astonishment as the doomed train, whose weight had brought down the bridge, careened into the air like an arrow fired from a weak bow, curving out and down in a graceful and strangely beautiful arc. Timbers of the shattering span rained about the plunging train; curling smoke from the locomotive stack traced a crescenting course toward the gorge bottom forty feet below.

The final impact was stunning: engine crumpling like paper, dust and dirt kicking up in an explosive cloud, flame blasting from the rupturing engine belly. The hellish sound of it wrenched unwilled guttural sounds from the backs of the Otie brothers' throats. In a little less than three shared decades of life, neither had heard anything to match that sound: metal slamming stone, wrenching and grating, wooden passenger cars crunching with the sound of a beetle squashed slowly underfoot, but with that sound amplified a hundred, a thousand, times, and made all the more horrible by the fact that the lives crushed out here were not insect, but human.

When the last car had fallen into the dusty swirl below the bridge, half-witted Canton Otie slid out of his saddle, staggered off to the side, fell to his hands and knees, and retched. He wiped his mouth on his sleeve, then retched again.

"Get up from there, boy!" said Dexter, without taking his eyes off the smoking gorge and the twisting wreckage at its bottom. "What you down there spewing for?"

Canton wiped his chin. "There's people on that train, Dex!"

"Well, I reckon there should be! It's a passenger train, ain't it?" Dexter replied, still staring at the remarkable and morbid sight. The gorge was to their west and it was late afternoon, so he had to squint against the golden sun to make things out. He pulled the front brim of his hat lower on his face for a shield. "Passenger train . . ." He paused, realizing something. "But not just any passenger train! No, *sir*! Sweet mammy, boy, you know what that train is? That's the special old Wilforth Bluefield runs in once a month or so, with all the rich folks who come up to his place to gamble! You saw that banner on the side, didn't you, a-flapping while she fell? That's the banner of the Bluefield Golden Special. I've seen it before."

"Think how they must be suffering down there, Dex!"

"Ain't nobody suffering on that train, boy." Dex often called Canton "boy," though Canton was slightly older than he. But only in years. Canton's mind had stopped developing somewhere around the age of twelve; to call him boy was not in every sense an inaccuracy. "Any suffering that's been done is over by now. Ain't nobody could have lived through that." Dex squinted harder against the declining sun. "You see any fire down there?"

Canton, making faces at the coppery taste of vomit that clung to his tongue, peered hard. "There's fire at the engine. Let's get away from here, Dexter. I don't want to see no more of this."

Dexter Otie dug an already chewed cigar from his coat pocket and set it in place between his yellowed teeth. "Fire at the engine . . . but not at the cars. That's pure remarkable, boy. Most the time the first thing that happens when one of these trains crashes is fire. Them passenger cars all has stoves in them. Maybe they wasn't lit this time. Or maybe there was safety stoves." He watched a few moments more. "You know, I don't believe that engine fire's going to spread to them cars. See? Them cars pulled loose as they fell and piled up *behind* the engine, 'stead of on top. The flames ain't going to reach them at all."

"Let's leave, Dex. Please!"

Dex ignored him. He gnawed at the stubby cigar. "No fire in the passenger cars . . . dead passengers, baggage scattered, a crashed train full of rich old snoots, and far enough from town that it'll be a good hour or more before anybody comes. . . ." He abruptly spat the cigar to the ground. "Get back on your horse, boy. We're riding."

Glad to hear it, Canton scrambled back to his mount. "We going away from here, Dexter?"

"Nope. We're going to visit that train."

Canton went pale. "No, Dex! There'll be blood and corpses and all. *Dead* corpses!"

"Ain't no other kind I know of. And it will be terrible, no doubt: brains, guts, cut-off arms and legs . . . but also bags, and purses, and jewelry, and baggage, and gold watches, and money pouches . . .''

Canton furrowed his brow, trying to think, a slow process for him. Suddenly he understood. ''You aim to *rob* them dead people, Dex?''

''Well, I don't much think they got need of their money and jewels now. Do you?''

Canton's face showed a mix of feelings—intrigue and doubt swirled together behind dull eyes. ''Is it right, robbing dead folks?''

''Boy, how many times I got to tell you: 'Right' is for old women and preachers, not for me and you. What's right is anything that puts food in our bellies, whiskey in our flasks, and money in our pockets. And listen to me, Canton: You know how the kind of folks that ride the special get their money? Off the sweat and blood of workingmen like me, that's how!'' In fact, Dex had never been a workingman in his life. He'd never been more than he was now: a small-time, habitually impoverished criminal who drifted around the country with a mentally impaired brother, looking for a big-time that seemed by the year more and more unlikely to come. ''There's money to be had in that train, and if we get down there, fetch it out, and ride like the devil, we'll be out of here before anybody else comes, and nobody will ever know we was there at all.''

Canton frowned. ''How does the devil ride, Dex?''

''Fast, hard, and he don't quit for nothing. Like the way we ride when the law's after us.''

Canton grinned, nodding, showing the wide gap where his front teeth had been up until three years before, when a drunk in a West Texas saloon had knocked them out with one blow of his fist. Dex had responded by beating the fellow severely with the butt of his pistol, leaving the drunk with a head that looked like a half-crushed melon. Canton had cried and pleaded for mercy for the fellow even as Dex beat him. That was just the way Canton was. Dex couldn't figure why. Tenderness was no virtue in Dex's view of the world.

Canton's grin faltered. "But the dead men, and the blood and all . . . I don't like to be around dead men."

"Boy, if there's one kind of man in this world who can't hurt you, it's a dead man. It's the live ones you got to worry about. Dead folks are just, well, dead. Harmless. Them people in that train can't do us no hurt, but what's in their pockets and bags and such can do us a world of good. So let's go. Show me how you can ride like the devil, boy!"

They set off toward the gorge. The sun was spreading wide, preparing to set, and its delicate end-of-day light cast the burning, ruined engine and the smashed cars behind it in a deep gold—Dexter Otie's favorite color.

Canton's nerve failed him when it came time to enter the one passenger car that was sufficiently intact to be entered at all. The other three cars were flattened, ruined things; through gaps in the wreckage, terrible sights presented themselves. A dead face stared through one shattered window; it was the sight of this that made Canton declare he couldn't go in. Dex would have to plunder the railroad car alone.

Secretly, this suited Dex. Alone he could take the biggest watches and jewels for himself and leave the pocket change and trinkets for Canton. The disparity would go unnoticed, unchallenged. Canton wasn't only a fool, he was a trusting fool, especially with Dex. He believed what Dex told him, unquestioningly accepted whatever Dex gave him, and just as unquestioningly did without whatever Dex denied him.

"You watch the horses, Canton," Dex said. "Stay close by to hear me if I holler. . . . That car looks pretty rickety, and it might give down on me while I'm inside. If that happens, I'll need you. You stay here, keep the horses ready, and watch that upper rim there, in case anybody shows theirselves. If you see anybody, give a holler and I'll come out. And the story will be that we come down here to help anybody who might have lived through it. You understand?''

"Yes. Is there any of the folks on this train still living, Dex?''

"Listen. You hear anything? Any voices?''

Canton cocked his head. "No.''

"That means they're dead. Anybody still living would be hurt and yelling. No yells, no live folks.''

Canton bit his lip and looked upset.

"Listen to me, Canton, don't you go feeling bad for these folks. Everybody's got to die sometime, and there's worse ways than having it happen fast, like it did to these folks. These was well-off folks—you don't ride the Golden Special unless you got money. They lived the high life and didn't die suffering, like Maw and Pap did. These folks lived better in a month than what most of us live in our whole lives. Don't be feeling sorry for them.''

Canton nodded.

Dex patted his half-witted brother's whiskered cheek gently and smiled. "Keep a good watch, and I'll be back out quick as I can.''

"You're brave, Dex.''

"That's right. I'm brave, and smart, and you'll be fine as long as you stay with me and always do what I say.'' He patted Canton's cheek again. "I'll be back real soon, with money and jewels and no telling what all.''

He had to climb on heaped wreckage to reach the half-intact railroad car, which teetered at an unnerving angle atop another railroad car that it had flattened. Dex, more squeamish than he would let on to Canton, couldn't hold back from one glance into the flattened lower car as he climbed past it, and the human ruin he saw—four men, as best he could tell, compressed into a space hardly big enough to accommodate one—was enough to make him wish he hadn't looked. He hoped the corpses in the upper car would be in better condition.

He clambered up toward that car's rear platform, watching his footing, keeping an eye on the flames gutting the smashed locomotive. As he had anticipated, they didn't seem to be threatening the railroad cars. Grunting, straining, Dex reached up and got a grip on the platform railing. He pulled up and made it on, and stood there puffing. Glancing down at Canton, he grinned and stuck a thumb upward. Canton grinned, but looked scared.

The door into the car was damaged, but the latch still worked. Pulling the door up and back, he looked into the shadowed interior.

He stared, and for a moment almost dropped the notion of going in. The dead might be the least dangerous people, as he had told Canton, but they were surely also the most unappealing.

The nearest of the several dead bodies was that of a man whose neck apparently had been broken as he was thrown about the car. He now lay draped over a seat, arms spread wide, a look of astonishment on his face, his head twisted almost completely backward and tilting wildly to the side at an impossible angle, making him stare at the next dead body, that of a plump woman impaled in midchest upon a shard of jagged metal. Dex winced at the sight, but noticed as he did so that she wore a fine-looking jeweled necklace about her neck.

Pushing aside repugnance, Dex made his way inside and began searching the corpses. He found a wallet in the coat pocket of the man with the surprised look and broken neck, plus a sizable wad of bills in one of the pockets, and gold coins in a money belt around his

15

plump waist. A good watch, as well, and a ring of gold and ruby. And a silver folding knife . . . this Dex almost passed up, then took when he realized he could give it to Canton as part of his share, and Canton would think himself well-treated for it. Sometimes it was handy to have a half-wit for a brother, a man who was glad to leave the money to Dex as long as he got a few trinkets.

Dex pocketed his take and moved on to the impaled woman. Working with his face twisted in disgust, he took the necklace, a matching bracelet, and several hundred dollars in cash stashed in a hidden pocket in her dress. There was some blood on the money, but he didn't care. He'd wash it off sometime later and hang the bills to dry like laundry.

The car moved beneath him as he proceeded to the next corpse. Gasping, he grabbed at the nearest handhold and almost panicked. What if the car rolled off? He'd be tossed about in here, with these corpses, and possibly become a corpse himself. He stood stock-still, hardly breathing, and finally chanced another step. The car didn't rock again; it seemed to have settled into a more firm seating on the car below. All the better. Heart pounding, Dex continued, robbing the purse and pockets of another dead couple, then three men who had been mashed together until they almost seemed one, then a pretty, young woman, not yet of marrying age, who sat primly in her tilting seat, eyes open, face expressionless, and not a mark upon her. Yet she was dead. He took her jewelry, her modest purseful of cash. A daughter of one of the older unfortunates, no doubt.

As he worked, he lost his squeamishness. These folks, the breed of people who would have never spoken to him in life except to tell him to be on his way or to get out of theirs, were in death now his friends and benefactors. What they had possessed was now his. What he wanted of them they had no choice but to give. It gave him a rather heady feeling.

He glanced out the window, saw Canton there below, still with the horses. He waved, but Canton didn't wave back. Couldn't see him through the window, probably.

Dex turned to leave the car, thinking that now that he had his squeamishness under control, maybe he ought to consider looking into some of those flattened cars after all, just in case a stray severed arm with an expensive bracelet might happen to be in reach.

His foot caught against something and he staggered, almost falling. Swearing, he looked down and saw that he had hooked his heel against the handle of a man's valise of some sort. Fancy leather handle that looked like ivory. He righted himself, reached down, and picked the valise up. It had a bit of heft to it. Interesting . . .

Pulling out his pistol, he held it by the barrel and hammered the lock with the butt. It held for a few licks, then gave way. He opened the valise and his eyes went wide, then almost filled with tears at the sheer beauty of what he saw within.

Bills. Bound and stacked. Mostly hundred-dollar denominations. Thousands of dollars. Wealth beyond anything he had ever seen.

He holstered his pistol, closed the valise, and bit his trembling lip. A tear ran down his dirty cheek and soaked into his beard. "Thank you, Lord," he said. It was, perhaps, the first time in his life he had said a real and sincere prayer.

Dex held the valise against his body and prepared again to leave. Yet once again his foot snagged something, and this time he fell completely. When he tried to get up, he found his foot was still caught. He looked down, and let out a yell of pure fright.

A hand gripped his ankle. A bloody hand, attached to

17

an arm that extended out from beneath a shattered, pad-
ded seat—an arm and hand that had appeared dead moments before, but now showed themselves alive and
strong, holding Dex with a grip of iron.

Chapter Two

Outside Bluefield, Colorado

The rider was big, with bushy hair that was still inky dark, though his whiskers and brows had gone stark gray three years before. Heavy, he was a daunting burden for his horse, which he urged on relentlessly along a wagon road paralleling the railroad tracks out of town. It was a strong animal, and still running hard, but soon the exertion it was being forced through would bring it to the brink of exhaustion. Jackson Murchison, though knowing this, would show the horse no mercy, because what compelled him to push it so hard was something that ate at his mind, telling him something was wrong out there and that there was no time to delay.

He had been resting on a bench outside the general mercantile in Bluefield, hat pushed low across his face, legs thrust out across the boardwalk, right in the path of pedestrians, when the awareness had struck him like a bolt. He had jolted up from his seat, startling a passing woman terribly and making the little girl who clung to her skirts screech and cry. The woman had hurried past him—people always hurried past Devil Jack Murchison—and he had set off for the livery to fetch his horse and begin this ride.

Something had happened out there. Something bad, something involving Wade, his brother and only friend, the only human being on the face of the globe whom he loved or, for that matter, for whom he felt the slightest personal concern. Except for his brother, he loathed the human race, and let the loathing show. Folks hadn't taken to calling him "Devil Jack" for nothing. He rather liked the nickname.

He'd experienced such bursts of extraordinary cognition at various times throughout his life, always in situations involving his brother. He'd never been wrong. In boyhood, Wade had been injured in a riding accident; Jack, fishing in a creek a mile away, had known at once, unexplainably, that his brother was hurt, had cast down his line, and run straight to him. And there was the time they had been hiding out from the law together in a remote mountain cabin in Colorado. Jack had been hunting when something had told him, urgently, that he must return to his brother at the cabin. He'd done so, covering three miles of snowy mountain country in an unbroken hard lope. At the cabin he'd found Wade suffering from one of those quick-rising high fevers that had plagued him since childhood. Using snow, Jack had cooled him and saved his life.

That voice that spoke to him, that bond of unexplainable mental communication he held with his brother, could be trusted. And right now it was telling him that Wade needed him, desperately.

And so he rode, heading out of town, along the tracks, toward the Bluefield Gorge.

* * *

Comprehension of what held his ankle caused Dex to yell and give another jerk of his leg. Still the hand gripped. Dex panicked: Sweat broke out on his forehead, his heart abruptly beginning to hammer . . .

For a moment he was like a man who had encountered a phantom on a dark road: paralyzed, filled with a primal terror that rationality could not overwhelm. But he did not let go of the valise of cash.

He swore and yelled again, pulled all the harder, and this time, suddenly, his ankle came free. Dex stumbled away, sidewise, up the tilted walkway, almost falling over one of the corpses, trodding on the arm of another.

"Please . . ." It was a man's voice, the man who had held him, and whom Dex now saw was pinned in the rubble. The bloodied hand groped out, fingers curved, and now Dex saw the face, equally covered in gore, the mouth open and begging in a coarse voice. "Please, get me out of here! You can have the money . . . just get me out!"

Dex sucked his breath in once, twice, and forced down his panic, meanwhile looking closely at the bloodied face, thinking that there was something familiar in it, and also in the voice . . .

"Murchison?" he said tentatively. "Wade Murchison? Is that you?"

The pain-twisted face changed, looked confused in the midst of suffering; the eyes focused through a red haze on the face of Dexter Otie.

"Dex Otie . . . Dex, it's you . . . I didn't know it was you . . ."

"What's wrong with you, Murchison? You caught there?"

"My legs, my legs . . . oh, God, I believe they're crushed, Dex. Get me out, Dex! You can have the money if you'll only get me out."

Panic was gone now; Dex's face was resuming its usual sly expression. "Wade Murchison! I'll be! Who'd have thunk I'd find *you* here, eh? Ain't that a boot in the butt, eh, Wade?"

"Please, Dex, help me!"

Dex dropped to a casual squat, studying Murchison, staying just out of reach of the groping, bloody hand. "In other words, Wade, you want me to do you a favor."

"Please, Dex!"

"Do you a favor . . . just like I wanted you to do me a favor once upon a time. You recollect that?"

"I'm sorry, Dex. I should have let you ride with us. I should have let you in on the robbery. It wasn't because of you I said no, Dex, it was your brother. We couldn't have a dummy riding with us, slowing us down. . . . Oh, I'm hurting. Oh, God! Get me loose, Dex!"

Dex, holding the cash-stuffed valise against his chest, cocked his head and grinned at the sufferer. "Now, Wade, give it some thought. Why should I concern myself with you? You sure as hell didn't care what become of me and Canton when you closed us out. Seems I recall asking you then what I was to do if you shut me out of that robbery. 'Wade,' I says, 'me and Canton have rid with you for a month, stuck with you, been true to you. What are we supposed to do now, you shutting us out?' You says, 'Dex, you can just go on to hell, for all I care.' Them was your words, Wade. Recollect 'em? 'Dex, you can just go to hell.' You said that. How long ago's that been? Five years? Six? Lordy! And you been in jail and out again since then. Time flies, don't it?"

"I was wrong to shut you out. . . . It's been years, Dex, years. . . . Get me free from here. . . . I'll let you have the money . . ."

"The money." Dex grinned and patted the valise. "The money. I done *got* the money, in case you ain't noticed. And I bet I know where it came from. That very bank robbery you shut me and Canton out of. The one you and your brother almost went to jail for. Why didn't they get you on that one? What did the papers say? Lack of evidence. I believe that's how they put it. Lack of evidence. If I recollect, they never did find the money." He grinned, patted the valise again. "I believe I've found it, though. Huh?"

"Please, *please* . . ."

Dex was enjoying this; Wade Murchison's suffering aroused no sympathy. He'd hated this man for years now, resented him. There had been a planned bank robbery, led by Murchison and his brother, raising high the hopes of a young criminal named Dexter Otie, who had tagged along with Murchison in some minor crimes and longed to fully join his bank-robbing band. But Dex had been excluded by Murchison himself—the most crushing rejection of Dex's life.

In any case, the robbery had gone off successfully without Dex Otie. Wade and his brother, Jackson "Devil Jack" Murchison, along with three other selected fellow robbers, had gotten clean away. Wade Murchison had been arrested at one point, but let go when no sufficient evidence against him could be found. Rumor had it thereafter that Murchison and his brother had hidden the money—a major haul, one of the biggest western bank robberies on record.

Wade Murchison, however, hadn't had much time since the robbery to enjoy his hidden illicit gain. While drunk, he'd robbed a couple of stores and a saloon, and gotten himself jailed for several years. Dexter Otie hadn't known until this day that Murchison was free again.

"You're right, Dex, that money's from the bank robbery. And you can have it . . . all of it. . . . Just get me free of here!"

Dex opened the valise, glanced inside. "Is this the whole take?"

"All there is left of it. I'd gone to fetch it, bring it back and split it with Jack . . ."

"Where is he? Bluefield?"

"That's right."

"Devil Jack's in Bluefield?"

"Yes, yes, waiting on me to get there. . . . Please, Dex! I'm hurting bad!"

"Ain't that a shame, now! Hurting. Legs all crushed up . . . phew! I see a lot of bleeding going on about them legs, Wade. You're going to bleed to death if you ain't careful. 'Course, then you won't be hurting no more, huh? All that pain will be gone. Whereas, say, if I got you out—"

"Please, Dex. I don't want to die here!"

"Quit interrupting. You always have been bad for being rude, you know it? Anyway, as I was saying, if I got you out of there, that pain's just going to go on. And then you'll go and tell Devil Jack about giving me this money, and Devil Jack won't like that notion. He'll take it back from me. Nope! I don't think so! I believe the tables have turned betwixt me and you, Wade. Now it's me who's saying no to you." He grinned and patted the valise. "Got to be going. Need to be out of here before folks come poking 'round. You know, I believe me and Canton might just head over to Goodpasture and spend a bit of this money. They got fine saloons in Goodpasture. And women, too."

Wade Murchison ground reddened teeth together; even in his condition, the fury in his eyes showed through the pain. "Damn you, Dex! Damn your soul!"

"That's a likely prospect."

"You leave me here to die, Dex, and I swear you'll pay. The devil will chase you, Dexter Otie! Chase you the hell down!"

Dex lost his smile. He eyed the weakening man, replaying mentally how this man had once rejected him for a robbery that would have put money in his pocket and made him a name among the sort of rough and rugged breed of men whose respect he craved. It would have made the past several years of poverty and drifting into something much better. Wade Murchison had denied him all that—but now the situation was reversed. He had Murchison's money, part of it at least, and it was Murchison, not he, who was in the loser's position.

Murchison began to curse. He cursed Dex, cursed Dex's fool brother, cursed his ancestors and his progeny. The words were vile, black with hate, spat out along with a fine, bloody spray.

Dex's fury surged. He drew his pistol, cocked back the hammer, and leveled it at Murchison.

Murchison snarled, looked back unflinching. "Go ahead and do it, damn you, if you're going to! I'd rather die by a bullet than bleed to death!"

Dex looked down the barrel, into the eyes. Part of him longed to squeeze the trigger. But he'd never killed a man before, except maybe for that drunk he beat in Texas, and he wasn't sure that man had died. He got hold of his temper. No reason to become a murderer now, not when death would claim Wade Murchison without his help soon enough.

He holstered the pistol, turned to go . . . then thought of another aspect of this scenario that he hadn't considered. Murchison might live until someone arrived. If so, he would tell what had happened here, how he was robbed, and by whom. The law would come after him and Canton.

He studied Murchison again, brows narrowing. The trapped man gave him back a look that burned to the soul, a look that put bellows to a fiery anger deep inside Dex. It was an anger that had come during a boyhood of abuse and neglect, and which had never fully left him, even for a moment, since.

"The devil take you, the devil damn your soul!" Murchison said again. Blood ran out the corner of his mouth.

Something inside Dex Otie seemed to break. Abruptly, he cursed, drew his pistol again, and leveled it at Murchison. "If I'm going to hell, you can go first."

The blast of the pistol was horrendously loud inside the enclosed car, the gun smoke choking and close. The sound made Dex jolt as if in surprise. . . . He *was* surprised. He hadn't known he was going to fire that shot until the act was done.

Dexter stared through the cloud at what he'd done.

He'd killed a man. Killed him in a burst of anger, in an unexpected moment of dark impulse.

He couldn't believe he'd done it.

He turned and retched, just as Canton had when he saw the train go off the bridge. This came as a surprise, too. Looking back at Murchison's unmoving form, watching blood spread out beneath it, Dex hurried out of the car, hugging the valise and eager to get away from this place of death.

Chapter Three

Outside, he found Canton with a face so pale beneath its leathery tan that he could make out the pallor even in the gathering darkness.

Canton spoke higher and faster than normal, falling into a repetitive singsong that was typical of him in times of fear. "What's the shooting for, Dex? What's the shooting for? What's the shooting for? What's the shooting—"

"Shut up! It was an accident. Pistol got hooked on something, pulled out of my holster, and went off. Come on. Let's get out of here."

Canton didn't seem to comprehend. "Who shot at you, Dex? Don't let nobody shoot you, Dex. You might die, Dex, and I'd be all alone. I need you—"

"Damn it, boy, I just told you, it went off by accident, that's all. Nobody shot at me. You understand me?"

"I'm scared, Dex."

Dex spoke slowly, softly. "Nothing to be scared of.

You hearing me? Everything is fine. Everything is good. Nobody shot at me. And I got us money, boy. Lots of money."

"Lots of money."

"That's right."

"Dex, are they all dead in there?"

Dexter gave a final glance at the car. "Yes. All dead."

"Is everything all right, Dex?"

"Everything's all right."

"Then why are you shaking, Dex?"

"I ain't shaking! Now, mount up, and shut up."

They rode off together, away from the wreckage and down the gorge, heading for the mouth of a trail that angled up the gorge wall to the higher land beyond.

Contrary to Dex's expectations, the fire did spread from the engine back to the cars, though far more slowly than in the typical progression of railroad disasters. Sparks were the culprits this time. By the time Jackson Murchison reached the gorge, smoke was billowing up and the gorge walls and tortured remains of the bridge were weirdly illuminated. It took a full minute, however, for the man to comprehend what had happened, and far more than a minute for him to find a way down into the gorge.

"Wade!" he yelled, fighting his way through smoke and heat. "Wade! Where are you?"

No answer came. Fire was licking at almost all the cars now. Jack Murchison put the back of his hand across his brow, squinted, and saw that only one car was so far untouched. That would soon change—a line of flames was crawling toward that last car very quickly.

Devil Jack, fighting panic, made a quick evaluation and decision. If his brother was inside any car but that last one, there was no way to reach him. So he could only make for that final car and hope that it was the one Wade was in.

Smoke was already filling the interior of the car when he entered. Squinting, holding his hand over his mouth in a vain effort to filter the fouled air, he dropped to a squat and worked his way through the car, looking at corpses, searching wildly for his brother.

He knew the odds were poor that he would find him here, poorer still that if he did, Wade would still be alive. But he searched on, clinging to that thin thread of hope. . . .

And suddenly, there he was. Through the light of rising fire flickering in through the shattered windows, through the dark billows of choking, poison smoke, he saw his brother's face. Wade Murchison was bloodied, eyes closed. Dead, most likely, but Jack would hope for life until he knew beyond question that his brother was gone.

Fighting for breath in the smoke-filled car, he tugged at his brother and found him firmly wedged. Cursing, coughing, he began tearing away at the rubble atop him, uncovering a dead man in the process and shoving him aside with ease. Jack Murchison was a physically powerful man; that strength, pitted against his enemies, had helped earn him his nickname of "Devil Jack."

"I'll save you, Wade," he said, voice crackly and tight because of the smoke. "I'll get you out of here."

He grasped his brother's form again, pulled, and this time Wade Murchison came free.

And groaned.

Devil Jack might have laughed aloud. His brother was alive! But hot blood gushed across Jack's hand, indicating some severe wound, and the way Wade's legs hung and dragged told his rescuer that they were shattered and ruined. He might have come too late to truly save his brother at all.

He began working his way back through the ruined car, feeling the floor going hot beneath his feet, the smoke becoming thicker, more toxic . . . and now the first flames burst through the car at the end from which he had just removed his brother. There was a crackle, a snapping, then a sizzle that he knew was flesh beginning to burn.

Fighting to retain consciousness in this hellish atmosphere, Devil Jack Murchison dragged his limp and injured brother toward the rear door and the open air.

Three nights later; Goodpasture, Colorado

Dex looked across the smoke-filled saloon, taking a momentary break from the pleasure of a good cigar, an excellent glass of whiskey, and a halfway good-looking woman, just to make sure that Canton was getting on well enough over in the far corner, where two bearded miners were cleaning him out in an obviously rigged game of dice. Dex knew the game they played, the game they were really playing: fleece the dummy. The dummy, of course, being Canton, who had no notion that his losses with every roll of the dice were as predetermined as the rising of the sun every morning. It didn't matter. Canton was laughing, enjoying himself immensely. That's all that concerned Dex: that Canton was having a good time. The money he was losing made no difference. Dex had given Canton only a small amount, and once that was gone, there would be no more tonight. Dex would dole out Canton's share a bit at a time to make it last. And Canton would lose it all, just as he was losing his daily dole tonight. Fine with Dex. The point of money was the pleasure it would buy, and since Canton wouldn't have anything to do with liquor—simply didn't like it—and since women would have nothing to do with Canton because he was a half-wit, what other kind of pleasure was there for him to buy, if not the brief thrill of gambling?

Dex turned his attention back to the woman with him. Her real face probably wasn't very pretty; the false one she had painted atop it with cheap cosmetics, however, wasn't too bad, especially now that Dex had a few shots coursing through his bloodstream. She'd said her name was Mary Alice McGee, and that she'd grown up in Illinois.

"I ain't seen a man spend like you're spending for the longest time, Sugarplum!" she said in a voice like clotted cream. The breath that bore that voice, on the other hand, smelled more like very old buttermilk, but Dex lived in an unwashed world of assorted stenches and didn't mind it.

"Hell, I'd figure you'd see big spenders every night," Dex replied. "Miners down out of the hills, bringing in their take to spend on a pretty woman . . ."

"Miners!" she said in a disdainful tone. "I hate miners. All I see is miners. They look the same, talk the same, smell the same. You, Sugarplum, you're different." She reached out and took the hand not occupied by the shot glass. "You don't have a miner's hands. You got the hands of a man who makes his way without slaving and sweating."

He grinned, sipped the whiskey, and tapped his forefinger against his temple. "Brains, woman. That's what I live by. Brains."

She glanced over at Canton, who was cackling in pleasure at yet another role of the dice and another loss of another chunk of his meager wealth for the evening. "Sugarplum, them dice rollers are going to clean your poor brother out."

"Hell, I know that. It don't matter. Look at him! That money he's losing is buying him a good time. And that's

31

what matters, eh?'' He stroked her hand and winked. ''A good time.''

''That's right. And with the money you got, Sugarplum, I can tell you that a good time for you this evening is a sure thing, too.''

Canton laughed again, and clapped his hands. She looked at him, then back at Dex. ''How'd you get a dummy for a brother, anyway?''

''He was born that way. My pap used to beat on my mother. I reckon he must have beat on her while she had my brother in her womb. I've always figured that's what rendered him stupid.''

''That's awful, a man beating his wife.''

''My pap was an awful man.''

''He's dead now?''

''He's dead.''

''Sometimes it's best that some folks are dead, don't you think?''

Dex saw in his mind's eye a startlingly clear picture of the unmoving body of Wade Murchison. ''I do think. Yeah.''

''I like you, Sugarplum. What's your name?''

''Don't need no name. Not with you.''

''I'll just have to keep calling you Sugarplum, then.''

''Suit yourself.''

The saloon door opened and a man entered, leaned on a crutch, swinging a stump where one leg should have been. Mary Alice watched him make his way to the bar and shook her head. ''Poor man! He comes in here a lot. I always feel sorry for him, losing that leg and all.''

Dex winked. ''There's worse a man could lose than a leg.''

But the mood for banter was gone for a moment from Mary Alice McGee. ''It would be an awful thing, wouldn't it? Losing a leg.''

"You ever do any loving with a man missing a leg or such?"

"No. I can't bear to touch a man missing any limbs. It sends sick shudders all through me."

"I got all my limbs. See?"

She stared at the one-legged man, silent, unresponsive, dragging Dex's eyes in the same direction. Dex studied the fellow from beneath beetled brows and asked, "How'd he lose it?"

Her eyes flicked back to Dex. "A railroad accident. A train went off a bridge. Just like that big crash the other day in the Bluefield Gorge. . . . Why'd you do that?"

He replied far too rapidly. "Do what? What are you talking about?"

"You gave a twitch, or a jerk, when I said that about the train and the bridge."

Dex didn't answer, didn't know how to. He drained his glass and shoved it toward her. She poured it full again.

"You did hear about that crash the other day, didn't you?" she asked.

"I ain't heard nothing about nothing."

"It was terrible. The special that goes into town sometimes, it went off the bridge, or the bridge broke down, or something like that. Anyway, the train hit the bottom, and all kinds of people died." She shivered. "It was terrible, the paper said."

"Huh. Yeah. I reckon." He drank some more, ready to drop this subject.

"Wouldn't that be an awful way to die!" she said. "Falling, striking bottom, getting tossed around and all, maybe getting parts of yourself tore off. . . . Oooohhh!" She shivered again.

"Why, them folks probably never knew what happened," he said. "What you want to talk about that for?

Me and you, we got better things we can be talking about. Or doing.'' Another wink.

But her subject held her captive. ''All those poor, poor people! Every person on that train died, they said. Except for one.''

''Yeah.'' He took another sip, then sat the glass down all at once and stared at her. ''What'd you say?''

''Just that I feel sorry for those poor people on that—''

''Did you say one of them didn't die?''

''That's right. That's what the newspaper said. There was a man who lived. But he was hurt bad, his legs all mangled up, and—strangest thing!—he'd been shot.''

Dex swallowed hard. *Murchison lived! Injuries, bullet, and all—and he had somehow lived!* ''Shot . . .''

''That's right . . . and you know what I think? I think maybe the bridge didn't fall by accident. Maybe it was weakened by somebody so that it *would* fall, and the people on it could be robbed. I figure that whoever shot that poor man is surely the same one who weakened the bridge.''

Dex spoke like the stunned and distracted man he was. ''That bridge wasn't weakened. It fell on its own.''

She eyed him, puzzled. ''How do you know that?''

''Huh? Oh . . . I *don't* know. It's just what I think. That's always been a rickety bridge. Tell me something, what was the name of the shot man?''

''Oh, I don't remember. I don't think there was any name given.''

''He's still alive?''

''I think so. He was when the newspaper was printed. Why?''

''Nothing. Just curious.''

''Do you know something about that train crash, Sugarplum?''

He slammed the flat of his hand down hard, making the bottle and glasses jump, making the painted woman jump, too. ''What the hell you asking me that for? Can't a man even talk? Can't he just ask a few questions, without some damn woman trying to make something out of it?''

''I'm . . . *sorry.*''

He pulled himself under control, realizing that odd behavior would only make her raise more questions. At the moment, important questions of his own were spinning through his mind. Was Murchison alive even now? Was he lucid, and talking? Had he reported to the law that it was Dexter Otie who had shot him—Dexter Otie, who had been fool enough to say where he and his brother were going with the valise of money?

This was bad. Very bad.

''Sugarplum, you're shaking!''

He swore at her, told her to get away, swept his hand across the table and knocked the bottle and glasses to the floor. As he came to his feet she did the same, backing away in fear, every eye in the place turning toward their table.

''Canton!'' Dex called. ''Come here!''

Canton wandered over, confused. Dex grabbed his arm. ''Come on. We're leaving here.''

''What's wrong, Dex?''

Dex said nothing more, merely hustled his brother out of the door.

Mary Alice, the painted woman, glanced around the room and shrugged. ''I don't know what I did,'' she said. ''I don't know what I said.'' She picked up her fallen glass and the overturned whiskey bottle, which was still about half full. She shrugged again, sat down, and poured herself another drink.

Chapter Four

"But why, Dex? I don't like being gone from you. I want to go, too."

Dex removed the gnawed remnant of a cigar from his mouth and, with effort, continued to hide his agitation. Canton tended to pick up on the emotions of those around him; Dex didn't want him getting upset just now.

They were in a small but comfortable hotel room, Canton seated on the edge of the bed, Dex on a chair facing him, pulled up close. He held Canton's hands in his own, like a parent talking seriously to a small child.

"Listen," he said slowly. "I need you to stay. It won't be for long. I'll go, take care of my business, and be back within two days or so. Maybe sooner. All you got to do is stay here in the room, eat, sleep, do whatever you feel like. Just don't go out. Wait for me to come back."

"What if I got to pee or something?"

"You can go to the privy out back when you got to.

Other than that, stay inside the room. And don't let nobody come in. There's plenty of food there on the table. It'll last you until I get back."

"Why you got to go?"

"Just something that's come up, and I got to take care of it. Nothing you'd want to know about."

"It's got something to do with that train, don't it?"

"Of course not."

"I dream about that train, Dex. And all the dead ones."

"Dreams can't hurt you. Dreams are like air, or pictures."

"I don't like dreams, not the bad ones. And I don't like staying in this room. Like I'm hiding. Is that what I'm doing, Dex? Hiding?"

"No, no. Just staying out of sight for a while."

"That's hiding. Who am I hiding from?"

"Nobody! It ain't hiding. It's just . . . never mind. Just trust me. I got to go do this, and then I'll be back."

Canton nodded glumly.

"Good. Good boy."

"Where's our money now?"

"Most of it's wrapped up so you can't tell what it is, and in the hotel safe."

"Is everything going to be all right, Dex?"

"Everything's going to be all right."

Devil Jack.

As he rode toward Bluefield, back the way he and Canton had come, Dex couldn't stop thinking about Devil Jack Murchison. It had been years since he'd seen the man. Yet he'd never forgotten him, and the horrendous thing he'd seen him do . . . and why Devil Jack had done it.

Wade. That was the reason. Wade Murchison, Jack's beloved brother. Funny thing—and funnier still that Dex had never thought about this until now—but the relationship between Jack and Wade Murchison had always been much like that between himself and Canton. Hating the world, cut off from the normalcies of life by criminality and attitude, the Murchison brothers nevertheless had enjoyed a bond between each other that was stronger than most familial ties. The powerfully built Jack in particular had seemed utterly devoted to his more cerebral older brother. He was devoted to Wade like a dog was devoted to its master—a devotion that could at times become ferocious.

Like the night Devil Jack got his hands on Pete Mims.

Dex couldn't recall it without a shudder. It had happened before he had been ousted from the Murchison brothers' gang, while the Murchison crimes were still minor and isolated, and bank robbery was no more than a still-unrealized ambition.

A couple of stores in western Kansas had fallen victim to the Murchisons and their hangers-on. Not much money involved, but it had been enough to tempt one of their number, named Pete Mims. He'd somehow managed to get his hands on more than his share of the take and make off with it. Wade Murchison caught him at it. There was a struggle, and Wade took a superficial knife stab in the abdomen. Mims escaped.

Though Wade Murchison seemed not much disturbed by what had happened—the money involved was minimal, and he was even able to laugh about the stab wound—Devil Jack Murchison set out on the trail of Pete Mims. Dex remembered thinking how glad he was that he wasn't in Mims's shoes. He expected Devil Jack to come back and announce that he'd found and killed Mims.

Instead, he came back with Mims himself, injured but alive, but surely wishing he weren't.

Devil Jack Murchison had carved up his victim pretty

effectively. No Apache could have done better. The nose was gone, and the ears, and the tip of the tongue. Thumbs, too, gone from both hands, rendering those hands virtually useless. ("Makes it hard to hang on to money that ain't due you, don't it?" Devil Jack had asked the sufferer, and laughed.) Long slashes marred Mims's chest, inflicted by Devil Jack's bowie. There were other injuries besides, but Dex opted not to see them. Canton, who saw about as much as Dex had, was sick for a week, and had nightmares for a month.

Mims was begging to die when Devil Jack brought him in. Brought him in like a dog carrying in a fresh-killed trophy, so Wade could see how dedicated his brother was to him, how sternly he repaid those who did him injury.

Wade observed the atrocity committed by his sibling on his behalf, and nodded. Devil Jack took Mims away after that, out onto the plains, and came back alone. Dex was glad he didn't know what creativity Devil Jack had applied to the task of finishing off his victim.

Dex had never forgotten that episode. He'd developed a terror of Devil Jack Murchison that day, which made it hard for him now to understand how he could have been so careless about not making sure Wade Murchison was really dead on that train.

He should have stayed long enough to be sure. That had been his mistake—leaving, assuming Wade Murchison was dead, but not knowing it for a fact.

After the revelations from Mary Alice McGee in the saloon, Dex had tracked down a copy of the Bluefield newspaper and confirmed that indeed the saloon girl's story about a lone, wounded survivor was true. Murchison's name wasn't given, but it didn't have to be. The story said the survivor of the crash had been pulled from the wreckage by his own brother, and was found to have a bullet in him. Who else could it be but Murchison?

The whole thing chilled Dex to the core. Particularly the part about the brother. Devil Jack was involved now. But how much did he know? Did he know who had fired that bullet into Wade, and who had taken the money? It all depended on how badly Wade Murchison had been hurt, on whether he was able to communicate.

Maybe Wade Murchison was dead now, and had never regained consciousness, never said a word. Dex hoped so. Prayed so.

Part of him wanted to take his chances and run. To assume that Wade hadn't talked and never would. But he couldn't do that.

He had to *know*.

And so he rode, heading back to Bluefield.

He reached the town by darkness. An odd town, Bluefield was, a place with two faces.

One was that of a typical mining town—muddy streets, roughly constructed buildings, storefronts designed to mask the smallness and humbleness of the buildings behind them, liveries, saloons, general stores, mining supply companies, an assayer's office.

The other face was more luxuriant, and set apart from and above the town itself: the big house of Wilforth Bluefield, the Pennsylvania-born barkeep-turned-miner who had struck the vein that brought the mines and town into existence to begin with. Unlike many such beneficiaries of good fortune, Bluefield had operated as a wise and cunning businessman, making his claims secure, investing his wealth wisely, securing for himself a life of ease in a big house, very nearly a mansion, he built above the town that came to bear his name. Beside it he established a gaming house finer even than his residence, carpeted with lush rugs, walled with expensive paneling, hung with chandeliers, filled with expensive gambling equipment. To this private gambling hall, inaccessible to the Great Unwashed of the lower town, flocked the wealthy and blue-blooded from miles around, usually coming in on the special train set up by Bluefield in cooperation with a fawning, eager railroad.

People who knew Wilforth Bluefield said he enjoyed living above the kind of common folk among whom he had been raised, and to whom he had slung liquor for years, before fate stepped in and handed him a fortune. He was seldom seen by the average citizen of his name-sake town, and those who did catch a glimpse bragged about it.

Wilforth Bluefield. Uppity, high and mighty, arrogant and better than others. Dex hated men like that, yet he couldn't wait to become one of them himself. Someday, he vowed, he'd live the kind of life Bluefield lived, and the bigwigs of the world would come to visit him, like those ill-fated blue bloods who had died when Bluefield's special plunged to the bottom of the Bluefield Gorge.

Dex wondered if Wade Murchison had known Bluefield. Probably not. He was probably on that particular train not by Bluefield's invitation, but as a paying passenger. Murchison had enough money in that valise to render him worthy of Bluefield's company, but he had never had the style of the upper crust.

Dex halted at the edge of town and dismounted. His horse was weary and due a feeding besides. He headed for the livery, then veered off. Best to keep the horse saddled and ready to go, just in case, not stabled away in a livery. There were things far more important to be dealt with than the momentary welfare of a horse.

Dex hid the horse in an alley, sneaked over to a nearby barn and stole a bit of feed, dumped it on the ground before the animal, and headed into the street.

Bluefield was not a particularly wild town, as mining towns went. The really big parties, everyone said, took place inside the walls of Wilforth Bluefield's big private gambling house on the hill. But still, Bluefield the town had quite a few saloons, and Dex made his way toward the nearest one. No better place than a saloon to find out information.

He paused at the window, looking into the lighted interior, studying every face he could see in the crowd. He was looking for Devil Jack. Wouldn't *that* be a situation, walking in on the man he most wanted to avoid! Fortunately, there was no sign of Devil Jack inside, and he went in, heading for the bar.

Dex seldom had much money, never in his life as much as he did now, thanks to Wade Murchison's valise. It felt odd to be able to walk up to the bar and order up a drink without having to calculate whether he could afford a refill.

Once this uncertainty about Murchison was settled, it was going to be fun indeed to be a well-off man.

He drank for an hour, striking up conversation with those around him, playing the unfamiliar role of the simple, friendly, talkative fellow eager to get to know those he met. He managed to bring up the train crash in each conversation, but found no one with information to help him. Disappointed, he headed out and to another saloon, a seedier place, where most of the patrons seemed farther along the road to full intoxication. Good. Drunk lips were loose lips.

He made conversation with a fat man at the bar, and found at last a fellow who seemed to know something worth hearing.

"You're right, sir, indeed. It was a tragic thing, that train busting off that bridge. Forty-two people died, sir. Forty-two! Hard way to die, that."

"That's the truth," Dex said, as idly as he could. "Not a single survivor, as I hear it."

"Oh, no, no, that's not true," the man said. "There was one who lived through it."

"No fooling?" Lord, it was hard to sound nonchalant. "Who was he?"

"As I hear it, a man named Murchison."

There it was. Confirmation. Not that he had ever thought it could have been anyone else. "Murchison. I don't believe I know any Murchisons. He's still alive, is he?"

"Well, I believe so, yes. Though he was bad hurt. Shot!"

"The hell! Who'd have shot somebody in the midst of a train wreck? You know, I'll bet it was an accident. Somebody's pistol going off while the train was falling."

"Maybe. Or maybe he was shot *because* he'd lived. Maybe that train didn't fall by accident. The notion some are getting is that the bridge might have been weakened by somebody so the train *would* fall. Robbers, you see."

There it was again, that faulty but sensible-sounding theory, heard now from two different sources. A wide-spreading notion, obviously, and seemingly one people were prone to accept.

"I see," Dex replied. "Don't seem likely to me, though. Weakening a bridge, causing a train to crash . . . nah. Nobody done that. That's been a weak old bridge for a long time."

"Well, whatever happened, somebody surely did shoot this Murchison bird, and he'd probably have died in that train if his brother hadn't pulled him out and got him back to town. He got him out just in time. Fire had spread to that car and would have burned him up in just a minute or two."

"Fire? No, no. That can't be right. The fire wasn't spreading—I mean . . . no, no. Never mind. I was thinking about something else."

43

The man gave Dex a peculiar look and said nothing.

Dex took a drink, pulled out a cigar, and lit it. He offered one to his companion, who declined.

Dex cleared his throat. "So, this Murchison fellow, the one who was shot . . . I wonder where he is now?"

"Why you want to know?"

"Just curious. No reason."

The man was different now, his expression and manner vaguely but disturbingly altered. Dex knew he'd blundered badly with that comment about the fire.

"I don't know where he'd be," the man said. He stood, and made a show of digging out his pocket watch and acting surprised at what it told him. "Well! Didn't know it was *that* hour. . . . Got to go. Got to go."

"Yeah. Yeah. Good drinking with you."

The man grunted but said no more, and hurried out of the saloon, giving Dex a quick and nervous backward glance as he exited.

He thinks I did it, Dex thought. *The fool thinks I brought down that train and shot Wade Murchison. And I can't much say I blame him. Me and my damn blabbing mouth . . .*

He stood abruptly. That fellow had left awfully hurridly. Just where was he going? Maybe to tell the law that there was a man in a saloon talking like he knew something about that train crash? Or might he be going to Devil Jack himself, to inform him that he knew where he could find the fellow who just maybe was the one who shot his brother?

Dex headed for the door and out of it, looking wildly about. He couldn't let that man get away.

There, down the street, he saw the man hurrying along. Suspicious, how he moved. A man with a mission.

Dex looked beyond the hurrying fellow, toward the other end of the street. By the light of a street flare he made out a small frame building with a long porch fronting it and a sign above. MARSHAL'S OFFICE, BLUEFIELD, COLORADO.

He was going to the law! Dex cursed and felt the impulse to run away, to find his horse and escape, fast. But no, no. That wouldn't do. He had enough to worry about with Devil Jack without adding to it the fear that the law was looking for him.

Swearing again, he headed to the darkest part of the street and trotted after the man, who was even now almost to the marshal's office.

Chapter Five

The knob rattled in the fat man's hand but would not turn. Locked. Dex advanced, unnoticed. The fat man peered in through the glass pane at the top of the door. The office was empty, the town marshal absent.

The fat fellow turned, sucked in his breath, and stood in shocked silence as Dex mounted the porch behind him.

"Howdy," Dex said, and licked his dry lips.

"Howdy."

"Come to see the marshal, huh?"

"He's . . . a friend of mine. I, heh, heh, I don't believe I caught your name there while we was talking in the saloon, friend."

"No, you didn't. I didn't give a name."

"Well, I reckon not." The fat man chuckled and made a pitiful attempt at nonchalance. "Well, the marshal's out. I'd best be going."

"Wait. You and me, we need to talk."

The fat man's grin was ghastly and false, maintained only with effort. "Talk . . . well, what about?"

"I want you to tell me something. Why'd you come here?"

"Me? Oh, well, you know, Bluefield is a good town, mines thriving pretty well. I had an opportunity to buy into a store here, and—"

"I ain't talking about that. You know what I mean. Why'd you come *here*?" Dex rapped the porch with the toe of his right boot.

"Oh . . . the marshal being a friend of mine, just wanted to pass some time with him. That's all."

"What's his name?"

"Who?"

"The marshal."

"Oh. Brown. Brown's his name."

"First name."

"Uh . . . William. William Brown."

"Why'd you pause before saying it? Don't you know your friend's name?"

"I didn't pause!"

"Come over here, friend. Let's talk."

"We can talk right here, can't we?"

"Off this porch." Dex lowered his voice to a low and threatening growl. *"Now."*

Intimidated, the fat man nodded. Dex stepped aside and let him pass, then fell in just behind. "Yonder. That alley."

"Mister, if you have it in mind to try to scare me or hurt me . . ."

"Hurt you? I told you I wanted to talk. Talk don't hurt you, does it?"

"Just talk? That's all?"

"That's all."

The alley was dark and narrow. Dex grabbed the man's shoulder, felt him flinch. He turned the fat body

47

around and crowded the man back against the wall, putting his face close, seeing fear in the shadowed, barely visible features.

"Why'd you go to that marshal's office? The truth this time."

"I thought . . . I was . . . I thought it was . . . *peculiar*, what you said about that fire at the train crash."

"Peculiar."

"Yes."

"Like maybe I knew something about the details of that crash. That was what you were thinking?"

"Well, I thought . . . yes."

"So you figured you'd go tell the marshal that you'd run across a man who maybe he ought to go have a talk with. That it?"

"I just figured, you know, that maybe you knew something, had maybe seen or heard something from somebody. I thought . . ." He spoke a little faster all at once. ". . . that maybe you had met some person who had seen the crash, and that maybe this person you met might have even been involved in it, you know, and maybe the marshal might want to ask you about it, that kind of thing not being my place, you see. Mind your own business, that's how I live my life."

"It's a good way to live. So you figured I'd 'met' somebody. That was all you had in mind, huh?"

"Yes, sir. That's it in a nutshell." He smiled weakly, and forced out another pathetic-sounding chuckle.

"You ain't a good liar, my friend. Anybody ever tell you that?"

"Liar? Mister, I'm telling you the truth, the God's truth!"

"Tell me a little more truth, then. Where around here would I find the man who was shot in that train crash?"

"I told you before, I don't know."

"I believe you do." Dex pushed a little closer, letting

his hot breath gust in the man's face, pushing his own lean form against the pillow of the big belly.

"Well, I can take a likely guess. . . . There's no hospital as such in this town, just a couple of rooms up beside the office of Dr. Reynolds."

"Where's that office?"

"Above the apothecary. Down the street, on the right."

"The doc live there?"

"No. He wouldn't be there now."

"So if this wounded man was there, he'd be alone?"

"Well, I'd figure the brother would be with him. The one who brought him in, don't you know. Or sometimes the doctor hires out folks to sit up with sick or hurt people in the night."

Dex nodded. "Mister, what's your name?"

"Stewart. Theodore Stewart."

"Stewart. What am I going to do with you, Stewart? If I let you go off, you're going to run off and talk to people about me. No telling what kind of things you'd say. You seem the suspicious sort."

"I'd say nothing to anybody. I don't want trouble, and I mind my own business. Yes, sir. Just like I told you."

"What you told and what I seen was two different things. You was heading to the marshal's office to talk about me, and you and me both know you wasn't thinking I'd 'met' somebody who knew about that train crash. You was going to tell that marshal that you'd stumbled across a man who maybe was the one who caused that crash, and shot that man in the train. Am I right?"

"Mister, I'd never—"

"Shut up. You damn well know that's exactly what you was going to say."

"Please, please, mister . . . I swear to you, I'll swear on anything you name . . . if you'll just let me be, you'll never see nor hear from me again. I won't say a word to nobody."

"You swear it?"

"I swear it, swear it to God."

"If you go back on it . . ."

"I won't! I won't!"

"All right. Off with you, then."

The man turned to head into the street. Dex caught his arm.

"No, not that way. Out the back way."

"You mean the—"

"The back of the alley. Go out that way."

The man looked doubtful. The alley plunged deeper into darkness toward the rear. It was not an inviting darkness, particularly not with this lean and threatening fellow behind him. But he had no choice.

He turned and walked back toward the rear of the alley. He'd made it three steps before Dex lunged up behind him, before something swung around over his shoulder, then back toward him, and his throat stung and burned all at once and his voice left him along with his ability to breathe.

The fat man turned and looked stupidly at Dex, groping a hand up to his neck, feeling the wound there and knowing, even as he began to collapse, that this man had just cut his throat.

Dex stood over the big, settling body, holding the bloodied knife. "I had to do it," he whispered aloud. "You'd have told on me. I know you would have."

He swallowed, imagining for a moment what it must have felt like to the fellow, having his throat cut open like that. He felt sorry for him. Dex wouldn't have done it had there been another choice.

He wished he'd been more careful, talking in the saloon. He'd stumbled terribly, letting his familiarity with the burn pattern at the train accident slip. If he hadn't done that, it wouldn't have been necessary to kill this poor man.

Dex closed his eyes and tried to keep from getting sick. He resisted a notion that kept intruding, telling him that the moment he began to plunder that crashed train, he'd embarked on a course that was above his head and beyond his ability to control. Something dangerously out of his realm, and made all the more so the minute he put that bullet into Wade Murchison.

Murchison. He had to find him. Had to go to those rooms beside the doctor's office.

But what if Devil Jack was there? What would he do then?

He didn't know, but it didn't matter. He'd gotten in murder-deep now, and there was no turning back.

He dragged the corpse to the rear of the alley and hid it between a couple of rain barrels. It wouldn't take long for someone to find it come morning, but he anticipated being far away from Bluefield by then.

He'd never return again. No sir. He'd get Canton and go as far away from here as he could. Maybe out to California, or up to Oregon. Maybe down to Mexico. Maybe even eastward, off to New York or Boston or some other place a world away from this frontier, someplace where the crimes committed in alleyways in mountain mining towns had no reach or reality. Instead of gambling, drinking, and whoring away all that cash from Murchison's valise, he'd use some of it to set himself up in business, somehow. Get a good life going, something that would provide stability for himself and Canton.

And all that had happened in that dusty gorge, and in this dark alley—and all that yet might happen this night if he found Wade Murchison alive—all that would be forgotten.

It was the first time in his life that Dex Otie had found the idea of a normal, safe, mundane life appealing. But then, this was also the first time he'd ever put his knife through the neck of another living man and watched him die in a heap at his feet.

He rounded the row of buildings and came out a different alley, onto the street. Looking down it some distance, he saw the apothecary shop, closed now and dark, and above it a second floor, windowed, words painted on the glass. The third window in the row was dimly lighted.

Dex shivered, feeling very cold. Yet the night was warm. *Got to get hold of myself,* he thought. *Got to keep all this under control. Think about it, old boy. Think about what you have to do, and do it the sensible way. You've got to find out if Wade Murchison is up there behind one of them windows. You've got to find out if he's alive, somehow. And if Devil Jack is with him. If Wade's there alone, then somehow you've got to find out what he's told his brother, or told the law, and then you've got to kill him. If they're both there, you've got to kill them both. Somehow . . .*

Somehow. Too many somehows. It was all getting too big and overwhelming to handle. He played again with the fantasy of fetching his horse, mounting, riding out, getting Canton and fleeing somewhere into the vastness of the nation . . .

. . . and knew immediately that it would not work. Not if Devil Jack Murchison was alive, and *knew.* There would be no place he could hide. No place that would shield him forever.

He remembered the sickening image of Pete Mims, all the things Devil Jack had done to him. A man who could do that might go anywhere, to any distance and difficulty, to find the man who shot his brother.

"Got to go through with it, old boy. Got to try, at

least.'' He spoke it in a nervous whisper, trying in vain to bolster his confidence.

He walked around below the building, studying it. The doctor's office was on the end of the building, accessible from a long, rear, second-level porch reachable by a staircase leading up from the narrow street behind the building.

Moving as quietly as he could, Dex climbed those stairs and again examined the situation. The building was narrow and long, with windows on the front and rear of each room. Dex saw that he could peer through the windows looking out onto the porch.

He bypassed the first window, which opened into the doctor's office, and the second, which was covered on the inside by a drawn curtain. The third window, the dimly lighted one, had an open curtain. A yellow square of light painted the ceiling above that window, cast by a cranked-down lamp inside the room.

Dex crept to the window and looked in. His heart raced.

On a bed across the room lay Wade Murchison, on his back, a big bandage around his neck and even partly up his face, and extending down across his left shoulder. His lower body was covered by a blanket, but Dex could see the odd lines and bumps that marked the splints holding the shattered limbs in alignment.

He was breathing, though with evident difficulty. His eyes were closed. Dex wondered if he had been drugged.

Most significant of all, he was alone. No Devil Jack.

Dex squinted and studied the room. An empty chair sat beside the bed, pulled out slightly from the wall. The chair occupied by Devil Jack as he watched his brother? Dex couldn't know. Maybe.

If Devil Jack had been in that chair, Dex could only suppose that he had stepped out, or maybe retired to some hotel for rest. Perhaps he had been sitting up with his brother since the train crash and had been exhausted.

Now was the time. Here was the opportunity. Dex shivered worse than before. He'd already killed one man tonight. That killing had been unplanned, improvised. This one would be different. This was to be a premeditated killing . . . but if he did it right, it would not appear to be a killing at all.

When they found Wade Murchison, it would appear as if he had died quietly in his sleep.

Dex reached to the window and gave it a gentle upward yank. To his pleasure, it was unlocked, and slid easily, quietly. He pulled again, slowly, and moved the window up. Crouching, he slid a leg through, shifted his weight, and pulled the rest of himself after.

He was inside. Energy pumped through him, intensifying every sensation and sound. He was going to be able to do it!

Quietly he walked over to the bedside and looked down at Wade Murchison's face. Shaking his head, he muttered, "You're looking mighty poorly, Wade. Mighty poorly."

The eyes fluttered and opened. Dex was surprised by this: Murchison had appeared to be in a deep stupor.

For a moment the two of them stared at each other, silent . . . and then Wade Murchison made an odd, squeaking noise, an oddly rodentlike sound of fear.

Dex reacted at once, putting a hand over Murchison's mouth, pressing down, making the man's eyes fill with pain. The bullet Dex had fired into him on the train obviously had entered somewhere in his neck or upper shoulder; that much was obvious from the placement of the bandage.

"Not a noise!" he whispered sharply. "Not a sound, but one: I want you to tell me, quiet as a mouse, what you've told your brother. Any yell, anything at all but a soft little answer, and I'll kill you dead right here. You understand?''

Murchison's answer wasn't really made in a true voice. It was merely shaped by his mouth, which Dex read by the dim lamplight: *Yes.*

"I hear it was Devil Jack who found you. That right?"

Yes. Again no voice, merely Murchison's mouth shaping the word.

"Did you tell him it was me who shot you?"

No.

Dex felt a wave of relief. "So he don't know who shot you?"

No, Murchison mouthed.

Dex began to suspect something. "You can't talk out loud no more, can you!"

No, he mouthed.

"The bullet?"

Yes.

Dex laughed. "Well, skunk my cabbage, Murchison! You can't talk at all! Is that why you ain't told Devil Jack?"

New words were formed by the silent mouth: *Damn you!*

Dex laughed again. Mouthed curses meant nothing, held no power to harm him. What mattered here was that his secret had not been betrayed, thanks to the sheer luck of a bullet that had chanced to damage Murchison's voice box. . . . And now Dex would remove any opportunity for that ruined organ to heal. Wade Murchison would never speak again.

Dex grinned. "I reckon they must think you're doing pretty well, to have left you alone here tonight. I must not be much of a shot, Wade—I'd really thought I'd shot you fatal there on that train, not just grazed over your throat! Don't matter now, though. Don't matter now.''

He yanked the pillow from beneath Murchison's head and pressed it across the face, positioning himself to put an elbow against the helpless man's throat, too, just to make sure the job was thoroughly done this time.

He pressed for a long, long time, until all struggle and writhing ceased, until the chest was unmoving. After that he pressed another five minutes, just to be certain, and then removed the pillow. Examining Murchison's face, he watched for signs of breath, of returning life. He felt the chest for a heartbeat, the wrist for a pulse. Nothing.

Wade Murchison was dead, and nobody knew that Dex Otie had killed him. Nobody! Not even Canton knew it. And now the secret was safe forevermore.

Filled with a relief beyond anything he had ever known, Dex headed back to the window and out again, pausing only to look back once at Murchison's still form. He grinned. "Sorry 'bout that, Wade. I'll be sure to use some of that money you left me to buy a few rounds in honor of your memory. My best to Devil Jack."

He slipped away, his mind now on recovering his horse and getting out of town as quickly as possible, and thus, in his distraction, failing to notice what lay on the table beside Murchison's bed, ironically pointed at by the curved forefinger of the dead man's left hand.

Chapter Six

He rode through the darkness toward Goodpasture, laughing aloud. The night around him was thick and sheltering, friendly as a warm blanket on a cold night. The danger was past. Wade Murchison was dead, really dead this time, and Dex knew he hadn't talked—because he *couldn't* talk. The only other man who might have linked Dex to the plundering of the train was dead, too— a nameless, fat corpse crammed between two rain barrels in a rear alley.

And that valise full of money, minus the little bit that he and Canton had blown in the saloon, was safely tucked into the hotel safe back in Goodpasture.

Life was good. And murder surprisingly easy. Dex, a virgin to death-dealing up until this little affair began, had now killed twice. He'd always wondered if he could. Now he knew. Killing wasn't hard to do at all. Just a twist of a knife, a bit of pressure against a pillow . . .

The panic came from nowhere, unheralded. It hit Dex

somewhere in the pit of his belly and made him yank his weary horse to a halt and lean forward over the big maned neck. Suddenly the night was heavy and oppressive, dangerous, poison. Dex slid out of the saddle and staggered off to the roadside, gripping his belly, trying not to become sick, feeling as if every bad thing in the world was about to descend on him. He had never known such a pure, unfettered, generalized fear. He huddled in the night, facedown, stomach wrenching . . .

And then the moment passed. Not as abruptly as it had come, but relatively swiftly. The night ceased to be threatening, the fear faded away, the pulsebeat slowed. Dex sucked in air, staring between his hands at the ground inches in front of his nose.

He chuckled. "I'll be!" he muttered weakly. "Did you see yourself, old boy? Did you see yourself just then? Whew!"

He rose slowly, looking around at the empty land, glad no one had seen him, glad again for the shielding darkness. Suddenly the earlier giddiness returned, and he laughed convulsively. Yet with the laughter came tears. He didn't know what to feel, what to think, and so he was feeling everything, and thinking in a murk.

He fell to his knees and let his emotions expend themselves, a mixture of laughter and weeping, fear and relief. His horse, puzzled but no doubt glad for the rest, watched him from over in the darkness.

At length he stood, wiping his face and blubbering. Sucking in a shaky breath, he brought himself under control and made himself think. What had just happened here, though strange and privately embarrassing, was nothing surprising. He'd killed two men! He'd crossed a line that he could never uncross. He'd moved into a level of criminality and guilt far higher than any he had occupied before.

No wonder he didn't quite know how to react.

And if he didn't know, then surely Canton would know even less. Canton. The one person, besides himself, whom Dex cared about. The one person who managed to maintain a perpetual innocence. Innocence . . . that was Canton. Even riding with criminals, taking his meager bit of stolen gain when it came his way, even then he never seemed to lose his innocence. Because Canton didn't really understand crime. He didn't know guilt, and so guilt never seemed to know him.

Dex decided then to never let Canton learn the truth. Poor Canton would never understand murder. He'd never comprehend why Dex had had to put that knife in a stranger's throat, and press a pillow over the face of a man already sorely wounded. Such things were beyond him.

He'd let Canton enjoy the benefits of the money they now had, his little games of dice, the food and candy and sweets that were his greatest pleasures. He needn't ever know all the ugliness that lay in the background of it all.

Dex could handle that alone. He was tough, gritty, capable. He'd killed men. He was strong. He could bear the weight of the guilt.

He headed back toward his horse, wanting to get back to Goodpasture by dawn. Mounting, he drew up straight in the saddle, sucked in a deep breath.

Yes, he was strong. He could bear the weight.

Reynolds, the young Bluefield physician, licked his lips again and stared at the unspeaking man who leaned over the bed, closely examining the corpse that lay on it. The room was shadowed, lit only by the morning light that came in through the windows.

"Mr. Murchison, sir, I want to assure you again that I had no notion—no reason at all to suspect—that your brother was in such a condition that this could have happened. Otherwise, I assure you, I would not have left him alone.'' He cleared his throat nervously. Jack Murchison did not move or respond. ''Your brother was in no mortal danger that I could detect. Broken legs, bruises and contusions, and a nonlethal, grazing bullet wound in the throat . . . but I swear to you, sir, I could not see then, nor now for that matter, any reason he should have died. It mystifies me, sir, and troubles me greatly. I wish I had arranged for there to be someone with him . . .'' He paused, debating whether he dared say the next portion, then did. ''. . . or that you had done the same. I had assumed, in fact, that you were to be with him last night.''

''You assumed no such a damn thing, Doctor, and you and I both know it,'' Jack Murchison answered without turning around. He was gazing very intently at the dead face of his brother on the bed.

''I . . . well, sir . . . perhaps I didn't . . . you know, there was so much to . . .'' The doctor stammered away into silence.

''So why do you think he died, Doc?'' Jack Murchison asked.

''I don't know, quite honestly. I'll need to examine him closely to decide. Some internal bleeding, possibly. Perhaps a heart failure that would have come on in any case, whether he was injured or not.'' The doctor thought that one over and liked it. It minimized his own culpability in this death. ''Yes. I'm sure it must be something like that. I can tell you there was certainly no sign of anything like impending death showing itself yesterday.''

''So you've told me six or seven times now.''

''Why, only yesterday afternoon, your brother was writing on some paper. Something private, it must have been, because he hid it away when I came around. Well and strong enough to write! I couldn't have anticipated that he would take such an unexpected turn as this!''

''Writing? Where's what he wrote?''

"I don't know." The intimidated physician looked hurriedly about the room. "Why, there! Beside him on the bedside table."

Jack Murchison swept up the folded papers in a bearlike hand and tucked them into a pocket, then bent again over his brother and looked closely at the lips.

"May I ask, sir, what you're looking for?" the doctor said.

"I'm looking *for* nothing. I've already found it."

"What's that?"

"Evidence."

"I beg pardon?"

"Evidence, Doctor. Something to show how my brother died."

"What evidence?"

Jack Murchison reached his big fingers toward his brother's lips, parted them slightly, and removed something small, white, wispy. Then the same from the edge of one of the nostrils. He held out his finger, bearing what he'd removed, for the doctor to examine.

The physician leaned close and looked. "Why, it appears to be feathers, or at least the fragments of feathers."

"That's right." He brushed them off his finger onto the bedspread, flexed his fingers, then pried open his dead brother's mouth. Peering in, he nodded. "And more about the throat."

"Where'd they come from?"

"From the pillow." Jack Murchison pointed at the rumpled, out-of-place pillow beside his brother's head. "A pillow that was under his head last time I saw him, and now is lying beside it."

"Why . . . yes. You're right. What does it mean?"

"It means that somebody moved it. I doubt Wade would have moved it himself."

"But why the ingested feathers?"

"What does 'ingest' mean?"

"Taken in. Eaten."

"He didn't eat them, Doc. He breathed them. Sucked them in because he was trying to suck in air."

"I don't follow."

"Somebody smothered him, Doc. Sometime in the night."

"Smothered him! Good Lord, sir, are you suggesting that he was *murdered*?"

"I sure as hell am. Somebody came in here in the night, took that pillow out from under his head, pushed it over his face, and smothered him."

The doctor held an astonished silence, then his eyes widened behind his spectacle lenses and he took two steps back. "Mr. Murchison, if you're suggesting, sir, that I had something to do with this . . ."

"I ain't suggesting nothing. Should I be?"

"No! No indeed! But I'm appalled, sir, and confused. I and only a handful of others, all very trustworthy people, have keys to the door."

"Well, there's two windows, one of them opening onto a porch you can get to off the street real easy. Them windows have locks?"

"No, no. I must admit they don't."

"There's your answer. Somebody came in through that window yonder, while nobody else was in here."

"God help us! I'll go fetch the town marshal right away!" Neither the doctor nor Jack Murchison knew that the town marshal was at that moment already occupied. Someone had roused him from his bed not thirty minutes before, informing him that a dead man had been found in a rear alley not many yards from the jail itself. The throat had been cut.

"Don't go fetch nobody," Jack said.

"But if this was *murder* . . ."

"I said, don't go fetch nobody. You understand me? I don't want no law involved. I'll handle this myself."

Bewildered and intimidated, the doctor nodded. Then his expression transformed to one of suspicion, and Murchison noticed.

"I know what you're thinking, Doctor. Don't think it. I didn't smother my own flesh and blood." He gestured at the corpse. "This here was the only living person in this world I gave one tinker's damn for, and whoever killed him is going to have me, not the law, to answer to."

"I see."

"You'll write up a report of the death, and you'll say his heart stopped, all by itself. Or something like that. You understand me?"

"Sir, there are ethical and professional considerations—"

"I'll tell you your 'considerations,' damn it! Here's the only 'consideration' that matters: Whoever done this probably wanted it to look natural. Like Wade just died on his own. You go writing reports that say it was murder, and that's going to get out. Whoever killed him will crawl under a rock somewhere and never be found. I don't want that. I want to find him. Myself. I want him thinking he's got away with it, clean and simple. I want him careless and not trying to hide. You understand me?"

"Yes."

"You'll be a good, cooperating kind of fellow, will you?"

A pause, then surrender. "Yes."

"Good. Good. Now step out of here. Leave me with my brother for a spell. And not a word to nobody, not yet."

The doctor nodded and left the room. Jack Murchison listened to him clunking about in his office, heard him slide open a drawer, then heard the clink of a bottle against a glass. Drinking, this early in the morning, and him being a physician! Couldn't much blame him, though, under the circumstances.

Devil Jack Murchison sat down on the side of the bed,

his weight making the bed give, causing the corpse to actually turn a little toward him. He looked into Wade Murchison's face, with its death pallor and half-closed, cold-marble eyes, and felt a burst of grief and rage that spilled up through his gullet and came out in a sob. Jack Murchison cried like a child, leaning over, hugging his murdered brother, and burying his face against the bandaging that covered the bullet-wounded neck.

In the next room, the doctor sat behind his desk, listening to Jack Murchison cry, drinking his whiskey as if it were medicine.

Jack Murchison had never been much of a crier, and he didn't cry long now. Wiping his face on his sleeve, he remembered the paper he had placed in his pocket. Digging it out, he squinted at it, reading his brother's last words, his breath coming faster as he read, his fingers tightening on the pages, and trembling. By the time he was finished he was up, pacing the room, face blood red, fury hot in his veins.

Devil Jack Murchison let out a roar of anger, balled up his fist, and pounded a dent into the wall with one punch.

One room over, the doctor jerked in surprise and dropped his drink.

Jack Murchison strode to the bedside again and looked into his brother's face. He held the papers in his hand, waving them as if Wade Murchison could still see them.

"I'll find him," he said. "I promise you, Wade, I'll find him. And when I do, he'll pray to God to die, because anything he'll face in hell won't be half as bad as what I'll make him suffer. I vow that to you, Wade, wherever you are. I'll find him, and I'll make him beg to die."

Dex reached Goodpasture at dawn, and took the horse to the livery, where he roused the liveryman and had him see to the overdue care of the mount. The liveryman was none too happy to be disturbed before breakfast, but took a warmer attitude when Dex handed him a sizable bill and told him not to worry about change.

Dex strode slowly across the street, weary, but at peace. The torments and mixed feelings of the night had dissipated with the spreading dawn. He knew now that all was well, that he'd truly done what had to be done, and gotten away with it.

There'd be no devils chasing him now. It was over, and he and Canton were better off monetarily than either had ever been anytime in their lives. It felt good.

He entered the hotel and headed up to the room. Gently he rapped on the door. "Canton? You awake? It's me. Let me in."

"Dex? Is it you, Dex?"

"Who else would it be? You all right in there? Let me in."

The door opened fumblingly, and Dex looked into the whiskered face of his brother and saw the visage of a man who hadn't slept, and who had been crying. A lot.

"Dex, I'm glad it's you! Oh, Dex, I'm so glad you ain't dead!" Canton threw his arms around Dex's neck, right there in the doorway.

"What the devil's this? You been scared or something? Let me go, boy! I want to come inside and get these tight old boots off."

Canton didn't let go, and Dex had to pry him off, Canton blubbering and slobbering the whole time. Brotherly affection gave way to annoyance.

"What the hell's the matter with you?" he asked, pushing past him into the room. "What are you crying about?"

"I was so afraid it had got you, Dex! I knowed it ate you! I just knowed it!"

"What are you talking about?"

"The thing, the shadow . . . the devil. That's what it was, really. The devil."

Dex plopped onto the bed, stretched his back, and began

pulling off his boots. "You been dreaming, ain't you! Having nightmares."

"It wasn't a nightmare, Dex. No. No. It was too *real*!"

Weary, Dex rubbed his eyes. "Yeah? Tell me about it."

"There was a shadow, Dex. Big and dark, and it was following us. Everywhere we went, there was this shadow, and no matter how hard we would run, it was always there. It was trying to get us. Trying to eat us up. It was an awful thing . . . so real . . ."

Dex flopped back on the bed. "Don't you be worrying about dreams and such. A dream might seem real, but it ain't. It's just a dream." He yawned. "Besides," he slurred out sleepily, "what do you have to worry about? You know there ain't no shadow or nothing can hurt you as long as I'm with you."

"That's what scares me, Dex. That's what scares me the most."

"What are you talking about?"

"The shadow, Dex. In my dream, if a dream's what it was. You weren't with me all through. The shadow, Dex . . . it caught you, and once it caught you, it ate you alive, and you were gone. Forever."

Part II
Pursuing Shadow

Chapter Seven

Canton couldn't have done more to thwart Dex's attempts at rest had he tried. He paced about the room, muttering nervously to himself, frequently looking out the window, and most annoying of all, asking Dex every few minutes if he was asleep. Sometimes he asked if Dex was dreaming, and if dreams ever really came true, especially bad ones, and Dex knew that Canton was dwelling on that silly nightmare about the pursuing shadow.

Somehow, however, Dex managed to rest, and eventually Canton settled down, occupying himself for several hours with a picture book he had found in the hotel privy during Dex's absence. Afterward Canton fell asleep in his chair, and the room was quiet except for the pleasant background noise of the midday traffic outside, the music of a quiet but busy town filtering in from the street.

Dex awakened in the afternoon in the finest humor he

had known in years. A great burden had been lifted. The danger was past; Wade Murchison was dead, and nothing remained to link his death to Dexter Otie. No doubt it would be assumed that Murchison had merely succumbed to his wounds alone in the doctor's boarding room. Jack Murchison would mourn and curse and stomp about and threaten the heavens . . . but none of it would matter. He wouldn't know about Dex Otie. Couldn't know, now that all the tracks were covered.

"You hungry, Canton?" Dex asked, shaking his brother out of slumber in his chair.

Canton blinked, sat up, and rubbed his face. "I'm real hungry."

"Good. Because I'm going to feed you good tonight, Canton. Big old steak, fried in a pan. Eggs, too, fried in the grease of the steak. Your kind of food, eh, boy?"

"It sounds good, Dex. It sounds real, real good." Canton looked closely at his brother, and smiled, showing that familiar gap in the yellowed cornrows of his teeth. "You're feeling happy, ain't you!"

"I am indeed, boy. I'm happier than I've been in I don't know how long."

"Because of all the money?"

"That's right. We got good money now, and now that I've dealt with that business I had to do, ain't nobody going to be coming after it, ever. It's ours, boy. Ours!" He laughed and slapped Canton on the shoulder.

"Ours!" Canton repeated. Picking up, as always, on Dex's mood, he came up from his chair and bounced on the balls of his feet like the boy that inwardly he was and would always be. "Ours! Ours!"

"You ready to eat before long? There's a good-looking café on down the street."

"Let's go there, Dex. Let's go now! And then later on this evening, maybe me and you can . . . I don't know. Do something fun. Play dice together in that saloon.''

"Well, now, the truth is that we'll be visiting that saloon, sure enough, but I'll probably be busy there doing something besides dice."

"Will I be with you, Dex?"

"Well, no. No. But I won't be far away. I'll be upstairs. You'll be having yourself a good time with the games. And I'll give you enough money that you can drink sarsaparilla all night, if you want."

"You going to be with a woman." A statement, not a question. Dex frequently left Canton alone in order to enjoy the favors of a paid-for woman, and Canton didn't like it. Dex's presence was necessary for him to feel fully comfortable and safe.

"I will be with a woman. Mary Alice is her name. Same woman I was with in the saloon the other evening. But I'll just be upstairs there, in her room. That's all. Just upstairs."

"Dex . . . when you was gone on that business, what was you doing? Was that a woman, too?"

"No. It was nothing you need to worry yourself with." He grinned and patted his brother's shoulder again. "In fact, from now on I don't want you to have to worry about nothing at all, not a thing. From now on you'll have sarsaparilla every day, and money to play at dice or whatever you want. The money we got is going to turn things around for us. There'll be good times from here on out."

"But it won't last. The money'll be gone someday, won't it?"

"Not if I turn it into more, it won't."

"How'll you do that?"

"You let me worry about that. Now, come on. Comb your hair up a little and knock some of that dirt off your britches cuffs. You and me got a steak waiting on us on down the street.''

Later that night, in a room above the saloon

Mary Alice McGee nestled her head against Dex's bare shoulder, picking idly at a frayed spot on the bedspread that covered them. Dex was smoking a cigar, blowing rings toward the ceiling, a sated and relaxed man content with himself and his situation.

''I like you, Sugarplum,'' she said. ''I like being with you, talking to you. Loving on you, too. I wouldn't have hardly cared just now if you hadn't even paid me.''

''I notice you didn't turn the money down,'' he replied around the spittle-darkened stub of his cigar.

''A girl's got to make her living, Sugarplum.'' She stroked the hair on his chest. ''I sure wish you'd tell me your real name. I don't like not knowing.''

''My name don't matter. It's me you like, not my name.''

''Do you like me, Sugarplum?''

''I do.''

''Well, you know my name. Seems only fair I should know yours.''

He grunted and took another puff on the cigar, then flung it onto the fireplace grate across the room. A cheap clock on the wall ticked off a minute as they lay together, watching the smoke from the discarded cigar curl up into the chimney.

''Is there some reason you don't want your name knowed, Sugarplum?''

''A man like me, sometimes it's best he keeps his name quiet.''

''You're a bad man, ain't you?'' She stroked his chest a little more vigorously. ''You know what? I like bad men. Ever since I was a girl, I've always liked bad men.

My mama could see it. Used to tell me it would bring me trouble. But I liked that kind of men all the same. And you know what? So did my mama. She left my papa while I was still a girl, and run off with a man who'd been in the county jail for killing a bank teller. He paid off the jailer to let him bust out, and took my mama away with him. She liked bad men as much as me."

"Killed a bank teller. Pshaw! That ain't nothing. That ain't so bad." There was swagger in Dex's voice.

"You ever killed anybody, Sugarplum? Is that why you keep yourself so secret?"

"If I'd killed somebody, you think I'd be telling you about it?"

"So you *have* killed somebody! I can tell by how you're talking!" She gave a shudder of delight, and hugged him tight. "It gives me the sweet shivers, just knowing it! It's all so . . . I don't know, *dark*, and sinful, and wicked. It just makes me feel all quivery inside to think about it."

"I never said I'd killed nobody."

"Come on, Sugarplum, tell me . . . you've killed somebody before, ain't you? You have! I know you have!"

He tucked his hands behind his head, leaning back against the pillow and wall, and looked contentedly at a ceiling yellowed by the smoke of scores of other cigars, smoked in this same bed by scores of other men. This was Mary Alice's place of residence, but also her place of livelihood. She'd wandered into Goodpasture three years earlier, a lost and directionless young woman. Since then her life had been lived primarily in this room, the saloon below, and in realms of self-absorbed fantasy, envisioning for herself a life of decadent luxury in the company of a man who was strong, powerful, and deliciously wicked, and who gave her quarters far more palatial than this dirty little upstairs room. She'd been looking for the living embodiment of that phantom man in every filthy miner and bum who handed her a few dollars in exchange for her favor. So far every prospect had disappointed her, but she was still looking—and this nameless drifter with the half-wit brother seemed the best candidate she'd found so far.

"Maybe I have killed a man or two at that," Dex said smugly, thinking about Wade Murchison going limp beneath that pressing pillow, and the fat man dying in that alley with a blade in his throat. The horror of murder, the terror that had driven him from his saddle and onto his knees on the way back from Bluefield was almost gone now, obliterated by rest and the admiration of a small-town saloon prostitute. What little moral consciousness survived in him was secretly bothered to think that a woman could actually desire her lover to be a killer—a bizarre and morbid fantasy indeed!—but any disquiet this gave him was far overwhelmed by the pleasure of feeling her twisted admiration.

She kissed him and whispered in his ear, "Bad men are dangerous. I like dangerous."

"Yeah? What if I'm dangerous to you?"

"You ain't. Because I know how to please you."

"I can't deny it. You done proved that."

Her voice became softer yet, an enticing coo. "Sugarplum, if you won't tell me your name, won't you tell me where you got your money? Did you kill somebody for it?"

"You set on making a thief as well as a killer out of me, woman?"

"Come on—tell me!"

"Why you want to know so much about me?"

" 'Cause I like you so much."

"If you like me, don't ask so damn many questions."

"If I don't ask any more questions, will you let me stay with you?"

He didn't reply, not sure what she meant.

She pressed on. "Where you going from here?"

"I don't know. Somewhere I can live the kind of life a man's supposed to live."

"I'd like to find a better place. I get so tired of living in this sorry little town, this stinking old room! Sometimes I'd like to set a match to it all and watch it burn."

"Why don't you do it?"

"What?"

"Why don't you burn it down?"

"Why . . . I couldn't ever do that. Not *really*."

"Afraid to?"

"Well . . . yes. Of course I'm afraid. I'd go to jail if I burned someplace down."

"You afraid of jail?"

"Everybody's afraid of jail."

"Not me. I ain't afraid of nothing."

She shivered pleasurably again—just the reaction he had been aiming for. "I wish I was like you. I'm afraid of a lot of things. Afraid to leave this sorry town . . . by myself, I mean. If I was *with* somebody, though, somebody who was, you know, like *you* . . ."

He didn't quite pick up on her drift, distracted by the action of fetching a new cigar off the bedside table. It was nice to be able to afford good cigars, as many as he wanted. After biting off the end, he settled the cigar into his mouth, fired a match, lit it, and let the match burn almost to his fingers before shaking it out.

"I think it would be exciting, being with you," she said.

"You ought to know. You're with me now."

"I mean, with you for a long time. For good."

Suddenly what she was getting at broke through, and caught him with such surprise that he reacted without restraint, or mercy. He laughed disbelievingly and said, "You want to *stay* with me, for good? Why, hell, woman, what makes you think I'd want that? You're just a *whore*!"

The tightening of her lips and flutter of her eyes revealed how hard his words struck. It was as if he had kicked her. She pulled away from him, body stiffening, and left the bed. Picking up a robe from the floor, she threw it around herself, tying it tight as if in defense, huddling in it, her back to him. She went to the dresser and pulled out a flask, from which she took a long swallow.

"Hey," he said. "Hey . . . did I hurt your feelings?"

She cursed at him without turning around.

This annoyed him. He got out of the bed and slammed the cigar into the fireplace. Grabbing his clothing, he hurridly began to dress, muttering beneath his breath. She took another swallow and kept her back to him.

"You called me a whore," she said. "You laughed at me for wanting to go with you, and then you called me a whore."

"Well, ain't that what you are?"

"I'm a *woman*. You don't talk to a woman that way!"

His temper rose. "Yeah? And a woman, a *real* woman, she don't sell herself to every joker who comes along with a dollar in his hand."

She spun, cursing, suddenly furious, and swiped at him with something that flashed. A small folding knife, he saw. He stumbled back, barely missing being nicked.

He cursed at her, and she at him, then she lunged with the knife again. He tried to deflect it and took a small cut on the heel of his right hand.

Bellowing in fury, he stared a moment at the bleeding hand, then drew it back and swung it forward, backhanding Mary Alice across the face. She fell with a shout and grunt, losing the little knife, gripping her face, and he stepped around her to the door, clad only in his trousers, carrying his remaining clothing with him.

The door opened onto a landing overlooking the saloon below; Dex's exit, heralded by all the noise and cursing, drew much attention from the saloon patrons, all of whom looked up to see him emerge. In the center of the room, drawn there by the sound of his brother's voice, was Canton.

Mary Alice emerged behind Dex as he headed for the stairs, and began pounding his back with her fists, cursing at him. The men below hooted and cheered.

"Go at him, Mary Alice!"

"Let him have it, woman!"

"Tear his head off!"

Only Canton was distressed. He looked at the absurd little altercation with an expression of horror.

Dex swore, turned, and rammed his fist into Mary Alice's face. She fell back on her rump. The men below roared with laughter.

Except for Canton. He put his hands over his face. A low moan began in his throat, rising slowly, becoming higher and louder, until suddenly he sobbed where he stood.

Dex swept down the stairs, not even looking back at Mary Alice, who sat stunned on the landing.

"Come on, Canton. We're leaving."

Canton's question came out in a loud wail. "Why'd you do it, Dex? Why'd you hit that lady?"

"Shut up! Come on. Let's get out of here."

"Why, Dex? You shouldn't hit ladies, Dex! You shouldn't!"

"That up there ain't no lady. And I told you to shut up!"

Canton bowed his head and cried some more, but he stifled the sobs, keeping them in. Dex didn't want him to cry, and he always did his best to please Dex, even when he didn't understand why. Even when he was appalled at something Dex had done.

Dex grabbed him, pulled him toward the door. Around them men were still laughing, calling up rudely to Mary Alice, saying things that were ugly and cruel and worse.

Canton looked at her one last time as Dex hustled him to the door. She looked back at him, their eyes locking across the room for a moment, until Dex jerked him away.

Chapter Eight

She sat on her bed, wiping her reddened eyes with a shaking hand, sipping periodically from her flask, and wondering how badly her face would bruise, and if she would be able to hide it cosmetically. And she struggled with humiliation, disappointment, sadness . . . and anger. A deep, burning anger at the man who had rejected, insulted, and struck her down.

Dex. That's what his half-wit brother had called him. Dex. Probably short for Dexter.

She wouldn't forget that name. Nor that he had struck her, cursed her, and all this before the mocking eyes of others.

Nor would she forget that he had rejected her. After all the tenderness she had shown him, the way she had loved him and tried to gain his favor . . . and he had pushed it away with contempt. Laughed at her. Called her "whore."

She wouldn't forget. And somehow she would get

even. She steeled her expression. When she left this room, she would do it with head held high. The men who had laughed at her before would laugh at her again, just to see her . . . But she would not give them satisfaction. She would walk high and proud and tall among them.

Mary Alice glanced at the mirror, stared at her own weary face—marred now not only by the ravages of her hard life but also by the red mark left by his fist—and dissolved into tears.

Flopping over onto the bed, she buried her face in the pillow that had nestled his head. She had hoped he would be the one to take her away from here and give her better things. He'd seemed like the kind of man she'd dreamed of since the steamy days of girlhood—exciting, moneyed, and deliciously wicked.

After she'd cried enough to feel a little better, she began wondering about that pitiful brother of her lover-turned-enemy. Odd, it seemed, a man like Dex sticking with a brother who at best could only be a burden to him. Maybe, she reluctantly thought, there was at least a trace of goodness in the man.

It didn't matter. She hated him anyway. She'd cheer and laugh if somebody shot him dead. Under safe circumstances, she'd shoot him dead herself. He'd humililated her. Rejected her. Called her a whore.

It was one thing to be a whore. Sometimes a woman had no other option. Had to tolerate it. But to be *called* a whore was a different matter altogether.

She fantasized about standing over him in an alley, smoking pistol in her hand, smug smile on her face as she watched him writhe and die with her hot bullet in him. *Now who's the shamed one, Sugarplum? Now who looks the fool? Tell me, Sugarplum! Who?*

Only one thing about that dark fantasy bothered her. The brother. The half-wit. He'd screamed when Dex had struck her. He'd asked Dex why he'd done it. He hadn't laughed, like the others. He'd been upset, not amused, to see her mistreated. If Dex were killed, the brother would be left alone. He'd be sad and afraid. She'd find no pleasure in that.

She smiled, appreciating a rather pitiful man whom she didn't even really know, because in him she sensed what was at least an innocence, at most an actual innate goodness. He reminded her much of her own older brother, whom she had known only in girlhood. Though not half-witted, he had been simple, none too smart, but eternally kind and good-hearted. Innocent. Protective of her. Gentle. He was gone now, killed in a war that shouldn't have been, in a place she'd never seen, called Shiloh.

Thinking about him took her back to the days of childhood, when life had been so much better than now. She'd go back if she could. But the world didn't work that way. You always went forward, ever forward, farther from the happy past and into the uncertain future.

She buried her face in the pillow and cried again. The room gradually grew close and cramped, stifling her. She needed fresh air, but the prospect of running the gauntlet of the saloon below, hearing the hoots and taunts of the vulgar men who had been entertained by her humiliation, was too much.

She doused the light in the room, went to her window, and opened it. Quietly she put her foot out and onto the little ledge there. Edging along it, she reached the side of the building and took a leap across the narrow alley to the roof of the saddle shop next door. This roof, unlike that of the saloon, offered a way to the ground via a narrow staircase on the backside of the building. This was an escape route she'd used a few times before. The alley behind the saddle shop was always dark and empty. A good place to get away, think, and breathe a bit of air that didn't bear the stench of tobacco smoke and sweaty men.

She made for the staircase, drawing cool night air into her lungs and pondering how deeply she now despised the very man she'd been ready to run away with, if only he would have had her.

Dex stared at the half-empty glass on the table before him, flipping his fingernail against it against and again, listening to the faintly musical *clink* it generated. Around the glass, and the nearly full whiskey bottle beside it, was piled money. Money that had once been the property of a Missouri bank, then hidden away and later recovered by the late Wade Murchison, and which now belonged to Dexter Otie and, in much smaller measure, to Canton.

The empty valise sat at Dex's feet. He'd recovered it from the hotel safe after coming back from the hotel and the infuriating altercation with that conniving prostitute. He'd stormed into the hotel lobby, Canton in tow. Hammering his fist on the hotel desk until the short, spare clerk emerged from the back with a napkin tucked in his shirt and traces of a late supper still dirtying his mouth, Dex had first cursed the clerk's town, then his hotel, then his town's saloons, and announced at the end of it all that he and his brother would he leaving first thing in the morning, and would he please go right now and get that valise of his from the hotel safe.

Intimidated and nodding quickly, the clerk scurried off to do just that. Returning with the valise, he handed it over the desk to Dex, who caught in the clerk's last glance something that seemed hungry and knowing. Dex slammed his fist on the desktop again, swore the air icy blue around him, and said, "You been looking in it, ain't you!"

"No, no!" the clerk had replied. "Sir, I swear to you,

I haven't touched that valise since I locked it up for you!''

"The hell you say!'' Dex reached across the desk and snagged the trembling little man's collar. Pulling him close—almost dragging him off his small feet in the process—he went nose-to-nose with him and snarled, "If I find one dollar missing from that bag—one dollar!—I'll take my knife and carve you a permanent smile onto your ugly little face. You understand me?''

"Yes . . . sir. Yes!''

When Dex shoved him away, the clerk almost fell. "Good. Now get over to the saloon next door and fetch me up a bottle of whiskey. And a glass. Good whiskey. Hear?'' He shoved some money to the clerk. "Keep the change.''

Canton had watched it all, trembling and upset, whimpering like a child. He hated it when Dex was like this.

The clerk had brought the bottle as directed, setting it on the floor outside Dex's door, knocking, and scurrying downstairs like a scared weasel before the door opened. Since then Dex had been drinking, fuming, and playing in money. Despite his threat to the clerk, he wouldn't know if any money was missing. He hadn't kept close enough account.

"Dex?''

"What?''

"Dex, why you being so mean to people tonight?''

"What are you talking about?''

"That woman in the saloon, and the man downstairs. You were mean to both of them.''

"That woman, boy, brought her trouble on herself. She come at me with a knife in the room, then with her fists up on the landing. She deserved what she got.''

"But the little man . . .''

"Don't like his looks. He's like a rat. I believe he may have stole some of our money.''

"Dex, don't be mad no more. It makes me afraid. Be happy, like you was earlier."

"Here's my happiness," Dex replied, lifting the glass in one hand, a wad of bills in the other.

"I think I want to sleep now, Dex."

"I ain't stopping you."

"You won't leave me here alone, will you?"

"No."

" 'Cause I might have that dream again. About the shadow."

"There ain't no shadow, not in real life. I know you can't help being a dummy, boy, but I wish you could get it through your noggin that dreams don't mean nothing. Try having a few dreams about all this money we got, instead of some foolish nightmare."

"I'm going to lie down now."

"You do that. Get some good rest. We're leaving come morning."

"You going to sleep too, soon?"

"Yes. I'm going to drink a little more first."

"Don't get drunk, Dex. I don't like it when you're drunk."

"I won't get drunk. Now, go on to sleep."

But Dex did get drunk, and Canton didn't go to sleep. Not for long, at least. He dreamed again—the chasing shadow, the nameless black thing that seemed to be after Dex, and which in the end devoured him.

And left Canton alone and afraid.

Now Canton roamed the hotel room, pacing about, compulsively looking out of the window at the street, then pacing some more, wringing his hands, worrying without knowing just what he was worried about.

Canton trusted Dex, and believed him when he said that dreams were nothing to be feared, nothing that could hurt you. Yet he couldn't get over his fear of them, this one in particular.

It seemed so *real*.

Dex had fallen asleep at the table, his head lying on the pile of money. Canton leaned close and looked into his face. Dex was drooling. Right on the bills. Canton frowned, disturbed by this. What if those were some of *his* bills getting soaked? Canton, despite his mental slowness, had a certain sensitivity when it came to such matters. But Dex never seemed to care. He didn't care how dirty he was, how badly he smelled.

Canton had trouble understanding him sometimes. They were different, he and Dex, and not just because of Canton's lesser intelligence. Canton knew he wasn't smart, like most people. Like Dex. Dex was the smartest man in the world, as far as Canton was concerned. He admired Dex's wisdom. He respected Dex . . . but sometimes he was afraid of him. And horrified by some of the things Dex would do.

He stared into his brother's sleeping face and mentally asked, Why did you hit that woman in the saloon, Dex? Didn't you see how it hurt her? Why were you so mean?

He wished he knew. He sensed a disparity between the Dex he admired and the Dex he had seen tonight, knocking down a woman. Canton didn't know many of the rules of life—never had anybody but Dex to teach him, and Dex didn't hold to many rules—but he did know a man wasn't supposed to hit a woman, and he didn't figure the rule changed just because the woman was hitting you first.

Canton reached over and gently moved some of the bills away from Dex's face. Now Dex drooled onto the table, but at least the money wouldn't get any wetter.

Canton went to the window again and looked out onto the street. The saloons were still open, their lighted interiors inviting, warm-looking, making him think of dice games and big drafts of sarsaparilla. He loved sarsaparilla. Thinking of it made him thirsty.

Returning to Dex's table, he picked up the whiskey bottle and took a tentative sip. Shuddering, he put the bottle back down and strode back to the window, forcing the whiskey down his throat. It burned, just like the last time he'd tried it. He wondered how Dex could stand the stuff.

Looking out the window, he saw a rider coming down the street, through the darkness. A big man, on a white horse. Canton frowned. Something about the man seemed familiar, his slump, his way of riding. Familiar . . .

. . . and sinister. Like the shadow in the dream.

Canton closed the curtain and backed away from the window. He was afraid again. There was something dangerous and deadly out there. Canton didn't know how he knew . . . but he did know.

Dex was wrong, for once. Things weren't good. Bad times weren't past. Maybe there wasn't a real shadow chasing them, like in the dream, but *something* was. Canton was sure of it.

While Dex slept and drooled, Canton paced around the room, back and forth, back and forth, and didn't dare go to the window again.

Chapter Nine

Devil Jack Murchison rode to the livery and left his horse and saddle in the care of the slender young black man who worked there. Carrying his saddlebags across his shoulder and his Winchester rifle in his left hand, he strode out onto the street and looked around for a hotel. He saw two on the street, separated by only one building. Picking the one that looked the shoddiest, and therefore probably the cheapest, he headed for it.

In a room in the other and superior hotel, Dex Otie snored and grunted in his sleep, and Canton Otie paced back and forth, fearing shadows.

Devil Jack walked into the squalid room the dullard of a clerk rented him, and promptly tripped over an overturned chair. He caught himself before he fell, cursed, and felt about in the dark until he found the narrow, sunken bed. After tossing his goods atop it, he probed about some more until he located the room's only lamp, which he lit. Cranking up the wick, he looked about the little room and shook his head.

Terrible, having to live in conditions like this. He'd grown accustomed to far better over the past few years, living off that bank money he and poor Wade had shared. They'd lived well on it, but quietly and carefully; they'd made it last, not blown it all on orgies of gambling, drink, and women, like most would.

Like the bastard who killed Wade and took our money was probably doing right now, he thought bitterly.

One final cache of hidden cash had remained. Enough to support him and Wade for another year or so. Wade had gone to fetch it—and a collapsing railroad bridge and a sorry rat of a murdering thief had suddenly changed everything. Taking from Jack not only the money he would have received but his brother, as well. Devil Jack Murchison was suddenly bereaved, suddenly impoverished—and it didn't sit well with him at all.

He dug into one of his saddlebags and produced from it the papers he'd found at Wade's bedside back in Bluefield. Spreading them on the table under the yellow glow of the lamp, he read them again, beginning to end, occasionally wiping away an unfamiliar tear—how many years had it been since he'd cried, anyway?—and more often cursing beneath his breath.

Wade's painful chicken scratch told it all. How none other than Dex Otie, a worthless and unmemorable louse of a man, a onetime would-be member of the Murchison gang and a man whom Devil Jack had all but forgotten, had appeared in the ruined railroad car after the train crash. How he'd taken the money, how he'd refused to help Wade free himself from the rubble. How he'd taunted Wade about the money he was taking, how he was turning the tables on the Murchisons for their onetime rejection of him, and how he and his half-wit brother would take the money to Goodpasture and enjoy themselves. And then Dex had cold-bloodedly shot Wade and left him for dead.

But Wade hadn't been dead. Dex Otie's bullet had taken his voice, but not his life. Nor his ability to write—and what he had written would ultimately become Dex Otie's death certificate.

Devil Jack looked at his brother's final communication and smiled grimly through his tears. "You always were stupid, Dex," he said in a whisper. "And you still are. You should have never told Wade where it was you'd be going."

Goodpasture, Colorado. This very town. If Dex Otie had done what he told Wade he'd do, he should be here, somewhere, right now. With the money. Devil Jack's money.

Devil Jack went to the window and looked onto the street, wondering where Dex might be. In one of the saloons, most likely. If so, he'd be easy to find.

Jack's greatest fear was that he'd come too late and Dex had already moved on. That possibility had prompted him not even to linger in Goodpasture for Wade's burial. Reeling with the information in Wade's final letter, he'd hurriedly set up the burial arrangements, sworn the doctor on pain of his life not to reveal that anyone had helped speed along Wade's death, and come straight to Goodpasture, hoping to find Dex Otie still here, and no doubt oblivious to the fact his grim little secret wasn't a secret at all.

If Dex was here, it should be easy to find him. And kill him. He'd even kill the half-wit brother, too, just to completely close the circle. What was the fool's name? Canton. That was it.

But Devil Jack wouldn't kill either of them until that money—whatever Dex hadn't spent of it—was in his hands. Then, and only then, would he pay back Dex Otie for Wade's murder. And that vengeance, when it came, would be sweet.

He'd make Dex Otie die a harder death even than that suffered by Pete Mims a few years back.

If he could find him. *If* he hadn't gotten the willies after smothering Wade, and moved on elsewhere.

There was a mystery in Wade's death, a part of the story that Wade's final communiqué couldn't reveal. Somehow Dex Otie must have learned that Wade was still alive, and sneaked back to finish him off before he had a chance to reveal what had transpired on that crashed train.

It came to Devil Jack that the papers Wade had written must have already been in place at his bedside even while his murderer smothered him. In his haste, Dex must not have noticed them, else he would have removed them, and Devil Jack would have never known the truth.

Jack went to his saddlebags and pulled out two small revolvers. Good hideout guns, these were, easily hidden beneath a coat even in saloons and gambling houses that didn't officially allow arms to be brought inside. Just the kind to be of weapons he'd need to go manhunting in the dives of Goodpasture, Colorado.

Jack readied himself, hiding the loaded pistols beneath his coat. Leaving the room dark, he headed out and down to the street.

He searched for the next two hours, until some of the more sedate saloons began to shut down. No sign of Dex Otie. Jack hadn't seen him in years, but knew he would recognize Dex if he saw him. Canton, too. But neither face was among the scores he had studied surreptitiously this night. He'd examined each face he could see reflected back in every barroom mirror or peering out of the shadow beneath a low-hanging hat brim, and none had been Dex Otie.

He's done gone, damn him! Murdered my brother, took my money, and fled! I've come too late. The thought infuriated Jack beyond expression.

And saddened him. Apart from the matter of the money, there was also his brother's murder to be considered. Wade's blood demanded vengeance, but Devil Jack wouldn't be able to achieve it if Dex had managed to vanish into the vastness of Colorado.

Devil Jack paused at the edge of an alley to dig a cigar from his pocket and light it. Time for some hard thinking. Even if Dex was gone from here, it might yet be possible to catch him, if he could manage to anticipate the way he would think and the direction he would flee.

The former, though, was impossible. He didn't know Dex Otie well enough to trace his likely thoughts. All he knew of him was what little he recalled from their brief and unmemorable association several years back, and what he could surmise between the lines of Wade's scribbling.

Dex Otie had bragged to Wade about his plans for gambling and such, which meant he would be attracted to towns where he could pursue those vices most freely. Denver, maybe.

But if so, Devil Jack wasn't in much better shape. He couldn't hope to track a man down in that kind of city. And who was to say it would necessarily be Denver that Dex would pick? A man with a bag full of money could go anywhere—and though Devil Jack didn't like to think it, perhaps Dex had just enough cleverness about him to drift to some city that any possible pursuer might be *unlikely* to anticipate.

It all depended on whether Dex had any notion just

now that he might be under pursuit. And that was something Devil Jack couldn't know.

Obviously the possibility of pursuit had crossed Dex's mind; it was this, surely, that had drawn him to the doctor's chamber to finish off the job his bullet had failed to do on the ruined train. Jack felt sure that Dex hadn't seen Wade's written testimony on the bedside table—but had Dex detected Wade's inability to speak before he smothered him? It seemed likely, on balance, that he would have.

Which meant that Dex probably now considered himself free and clear. Having no notion that Wade had recorded on paper the details of his own shooting, Dex probably believed he had successfully silenced the matter forever when he smothered away Wade's life.

Unless somebody else besides Dex had smothered him—but who else would have done so? What would have been the motive? It had to be Dex Otie. It was the only possibility that fit.

Devil Jack puffed his cigar and calmed himself down. So he hadn't found Dex tonight. It was still too early to assume he might not find him later. Maybe he was in town, but not in the saloons. Jack glanced toward his own hotel. Maybe he was there. In some other room right in the same building as his pursuer. Then Jack's eyes shifted down to the better hotel, and he nodded. *That* would be the more likely place. Dex had money now. He'd pick the better hotel.

Devil Jack took a last draw on his cigar and tossed it to the ground, where he crushed out the glowing red coal beneath his boot. Feeling the need to relieve his bladder, he slipped down the alley and around behind the building. When his business was taken care of, he turned to go back to the street, thinking he might make an inquiry at that hotel, just to see if any young fellow with a half-wit brother might be staying there.

He was about to turn around the rear of the building and up toward the street when he realized he wasn't alone. Someone was in the darkness behind the adjacent building. Someone, he saw when he squinted hard, who wore a dress.

He'd just relieved himself with a woman right there to see it. It would have embarrassed most men, but it only made Devil Jack mad.

"What the hell! You always stand about and not make a peep while a man's making his water?"

"Mister, in case you ain't noticed, it's right dark back here. I didn't see nothing. And if I had, believe me, it wouldn't have been nothing I ain't seen a hundred times before."

Her voice, though unfamiliar, bore a quality that Jack Murchison had encountered often before. It was the tired, used voice of a woman who was herself tired and used, jaded and weary and worldly wise.

"Huh. You're a whore, I reckon." He said it flatly, a statement of fact rather than an insult.

And so Mary Alice didn't take it in the same way she had when Dex Otie had expressed the same assessment of her earlier this same night. She stepped closer to the stranger, to where she could vaguely make out his features. A big man, this one.

"I am," she replied.

"Ain't going to find much business hanging about in the shadows behind buildings."

"I found you, didn't I?"

"I found you is more like it. But there's only one thing: I ain't in the market for a woman tonight."

"And I ain't *on* the market tonight," she replied. "The truth is, mister, I came back here to get away from anybody and everybody, and if I stood quiet while you took your pee there, it's only because I wasn't wanting to be found at all."

He tried to see her better, beginning to be intrigued by her and thinking that maybe he might be in the market for a woman tonight, after all. A distraction might be pleasant after the disappointment of not finding Dexter Otie in any of the saloons.

A thought came.

"You a saloon gal, honey?"

"Yes. The Kirk House Saloon." She gestured in the darkness. "Yonder."

"I reckon you see a lot of drifters come through town, huh?"

"I reckon I do."

"Well, maybe you seen a man I'm in town trying to find."

"Maybe I have, maybe I ain't. Why you trying to find him?"

He might have lied then. It would have made sense, and been easy enough, but something in him, some instinct roused by a certain quality he sensed in this woman's personality and manner, told him to simply tell the truth. "I've come to get back some money he stole from me. And then I aim to kill him, to pay him back for murdering my only brother."

She didn't answer for a moment, and he wondered if his instinct had been amiss. But she stepped closer, reached out, and laid a hand on his broad chest. "You're a bad man, ain't you! You know, Sugarplum, I like bad men. Always have."

"I ain't surprised. And I reckon I am a bad man. About as bad as they come. They call me Devil Jack, and it ain't without reason."

"You got a room in town, Devil Jack?"

"Place in one of the hotels."

"Which?"

"Campbell's, I believe the name was. Shoddy place."

"I can make it a lot nicer."

"That you could."

"Can I come with you?"

"You ain't answered me about the man I'm looking for."

"If I can answer, will you take me to your room? I don't want to go back to my place tonight. I'm sick of being there." She gently rubbed his chest with the flat of her right hand. "I want to be with somebody like you this evening."

He reached up and grasped her wrist, but not roughly. "What's your name?"

"Mary Alice McGee."

"Mary Alice McGee, if you can help me find the man I'm looking for, I'll make it worth your while in every way there is."

"That include money?"

"If you can help me, and if I get my money back from this bastard, there'll be more money for you than you'd make in a month of rolling around with these stinking Colorado miners. But if you can't help me, then you're wasting my time, and I don't cotton to having my time wasted."

She twisted her wrist free. "All right. Tell me who this man is you're looking for."

"I ain't seen him in a few years, but he'd be a sandy-haired fellow, on the tall side, and thin. Got him a half-wit brother he runs about with, and his name—"

"Dex. His name is Dex."

A pause. "Yes. That's him."

"Mister Devil Jack, sir, you and me need to talk."

"I believe we do. Come on up to my hotel."

She slipped her arm around his, and they walked out of the alley toward the street.

Chapter Ten

She was pretty, in a tired and worn kind of way, but Devil Jack scarcely noticed. They sat on either side of the little table in his room, their faces warm with lamplight, and looked into each other's eyes as they discussed, in low and conspiratorial tones, the vile and hated person of Dexter Otie. On the table were the papers Wade Murchison had scribbled out in his last hours of life.

"He bragged to me about being a killer," she said, talking about Dex. "But he didn't say who, or when, or how, nothing like that. It was your brother?"

"Yes. You heard of the train falling into the gulch over toward Bluefield? My brother was on that train. He was the only one to live through the crash."

"Yes. I read about it in the newspaper."

"Dex Otie got on that train and was robbing corpses. That's what my brother wrote down before he died . . . before he was *murdered*. Anyhow, whilst robbing the

96

dead on that train, Dex Otie found my brother Wade alive, and knew him.'' He paused, debating whether to trust her with details of his past. He decided that he did trust her. ''There was a time when Dex Otie had rid with my brother and me, back in the days we did a bit of robbing. Me and Wade and some others was setting up a gang, planning to rob a bank. Dex wanted in on it. Wade said no. Sent him on his way. We didn't trust him, nor did it make much sense to bring in somebody who tows a half-wit around with him, slowing him down. We couldn't afford that risk. But Dex held it against Wade, and me, for cutting him out.''

''So when he saw your brother on that train, and found his money . . .''

''Right. He seen it as a way to even the score. Wade begged him to get him free, told him his legs were trapped. But Dex Otie just shot him. Like a dog. It's all wrote down, right here.'' He touched the papers.

''But that shot he fired didn't kill Wade. It tore through his throat and took away his voice, but he lived. I found him on the train, and if I'd got there much later, Wade would have burned to death.''

''How'd you come to be there?''

''I don't know. I swear I don't. It was something that come to me while I was in town . . . a kind of knowing. Knowing that Wade was in trouble and needed me. Wade and me, we've been real close. Real close.''

''What happened after you got your brother off the train?''

''I took him back to Bluefield, to a doctor. He patched up Wade's throat—though Wade still couldn't talk a lick—and splinted down his legs. They was all crushed up. And Wade, though he was hurting, seemed to be likely to mend. And then the doc and me find Wade dead in his bed. It looked like he'd just passed off on his own, but I looked close, and there was clear sign he'd been smothered with his own pillow.''

"And you figure Dex Otie done it?"

"Who else? I figure that somehow he found out that Wade was still alive, and got to thinking how Wade could tell what he'd done, and went back to finish off what he'd started.''

"Oh . . .'' Her expression and manner had abruptly changed.

"What?''

"I know how Dex Otie found out your brother was still alive.''

"How?''

"He was told it—'' She caught her words back just before she revealed the truth, realizing he might hold her at fault for being the one who told Dex about Wade Murchison's survival. "He was told it by a man at the bar in the saloon. I was with him, heard it all. The man had read about it in the paper. When Dex—I didn't know his name was Dex at the time—when he heard about it, he got up quick and left. He looked . . . funny. Odd. Like something was wrong.''

"Something *was* wrong. The bastard had just found out that he wasn't quite the clever murderer he thought he was.''

"Next time I saw Dex, he was different. Big spender. Happy. Paid me to spend some time with him up in my room.''

"He'd killed Wade by then,'' Devil Jack said. "Figured he was in the clear. What he didn't know about was this.'' He slapped the papers on the table. "Tell me something, Mary Alice. Do you know where he's gone?''

"He ain't gone.''

"What?''

"He's still here.''

98

Devil Jack came to his feet so fast, his chair tipped over behind him. "Where is he?"

"I can . . ." She was about to say *take you to him,* but across her mind came the image of Canton Otie, who had looked at her so sorrowfully and tenderly after Dex had humiliated her, who had reminded her so of her own dear lost brother. If she took this furious stranger to Dex, he'd probably kill not only Dex, but Canton, too. ". . . I can bring Dex to you. With him not knowing, of course."

"You sure?"

"No . . . but I believe I can. You said there'd be a cut of the money if I . . ."

"Enough to set your curly-haired little head to swimming."

"Enough I can get away from this sorry town, set myself up in a city somewhere?"

"Yes, woman! Now tell me what you've got in mind."

She lowered her head a moment, thinking. He waited, eagerly, fingers twitching like fat worms, the hidden pistols heavy beneath his coat, big heart hammering like a drum inside his chest.

She walked across the street, toward the Goodpasture Hotel, where Dex Otie and his brother were lodging.

She hadn't expected to be this nervous. Nor this doubtful. Now that she was actually engaged in carrying out this plan of her own devising—feeling the burning eyes of Devil Jack upon her as he watched from hiding—she was wondering if she had jumped into this scheme too hastily. What if she failed? Would this Devil Jack, still a stranger to her, believe she had betrayed him and punish her for it? She liked bad men, to be sure, but not when their badness made her its object.

The plan she and Devil Jack had agreed upon was

simple. She would go to Dex's room and tell him that she'd learned something he should know, something dire and crucial involving the crash of that train over at the Bluefield Gorge. A man had come to town, looking for Dex, bringing him warning that someone was after him. Dex wouldn't be able to resist investigating. He'd leave his hotel, go with her to where Devil Jack waited in an empty backlot shed—and then it would be Dex Otie's turn to be punished and humiliated. And ultimately, his turn to die.

She entered the hotel lobby after making some subtle glances through the front window to make sure the clerk was, as usual, occupied somewhere in the back. Her reputation was widely known through Goodpasture, and the clerk had a moralistic streak when it came to her profession: When any known "cyprian" showed up in his hotel, he made quite a show of tossing her out.

Mary Alice let herself in through the front door. Quietly she tiptoed across the lobby to the stairs and began to climb. They creaked more than she would have liked, but if the clerk heard it, he never emerged. She made it around the first landing and out of sight of the desk without his ever showing himself.

She climbed to the second floor. During their earlier negotiations over the price of her specialized transaction and where it would take place, Dex had mentioned that he was staying in a second-floor room at the Goodpasture Hotel, but hadn't mentioned the room's number. Mary Alice stood at the end of the hall and the four closed doors that led off it, wondering behind which one she could find Dex.

The second-floor rooms were all numbered beginning with a *B*. She went to the closest, Room B1, rapped gently on it, and got no response. The latch hadn't caught, and the door swung open at her touch, revealing an unoccupied room. No Dex Otie in this one.

She closed the door; this time the latch clicked. She moved down the hall to B2. This room, sound indicated, was occupied. Someone was inside, pacing back and forth.

She rapped on the door. The pacing stopped.

"Who's there?" It was the voice of the half-wit brother, the same voice that had pleaded for her when Dex had struck her. She felt a responsive, tender tremor in her heart.

"It's Mary Alice McGee. The woman from the saloon."

A pause. "Why are you here?"

"I have news. For Dex."

Canton's voice was quavery. He was upset and getting more so. "Dex can't talk right now. He's asleep."

"Can't you wake him up? It's important I speak to him."

"I don't know if I should . . ."

Mary Alice began to feel troubled. She hadn't anticipated having to deal with Dex's pity-inspiring brother. This cast a different light onto everything. It was Dex she hated and wanted to punish, not his unfortunate sibling—the one who so reminded her of her own brother, and thus touched the one part of her heart that hadn't become numbed by the life she lived. "It's important," she repeated.

She heard Canton urgently saying Dex's name. There was no response but a guttural moan.

I'll bet he's drunk in there, she thought. This was bad. If he was passed-out drunk, she'd never get him out to where Devil Jack waited. What that would mean she couldn't say. Devil Jack might punish her, or might come marching over here in fury and gun down Dex in his room, and Canton with him.

That prospect was intolerable. Canton was the only true innocent involved in this whole affair, and if she was a hardened, bitter woman, she wasn't yet so jaded that she'd allow harm to come to someone so much like a child. Especially not one whose face had been the only one among a roomful to show concern when she had been hurt and shamed, and whose voice had been the only one to rise in sympathy for her rather than mockery.

"What's your name?" she asked. "Is it Canton?"

"Yes."

"Canton, can you open the door, so we can talk?"

"I don't know . . . Dex might not like it."

"Let me see Dex. Maybe I can wake him up."

"He'll be mad. . . ."

"Canton, if you don't cooperate with me, Dex could be hurt, or worse. You have to believe me!"

In the silence following, she fancied she could almost hear the clicking of Canton's worried mind. Then his hand touched the latch and the door slowly swung open.

He looked closely at her face. "I can see where he hit you," he said. "I'm sorry he hit you."

"I know that you're sorry. I could tell." She looked past him. "Is Dex in his bed, or is he—" She cut off abruptly, having seen Dex passed out at the table, his head lying amid a heap of bills. More bills than she had ever seen in her life. She stared, unable for several moments even to blink.

Wild thoughts raced through her mind. She could rush in, grab handfuls of the money, and dart out again before this dim-witted fellow could even respond. She could leave the hotel by the back door, hide somewhere, get out of town any way she could, and let Devil Jack Murchison and Dex Otie work out their difficulties between themselves any way they could. And if Canton Otie got hurt or killed in the process, what was that to her? It wouldn't be the first time in this sorry world that an innocent had suffered.

"He's drunk," Canton said. "He told me he wouldn't

get drunk, but he did. I don't like it when he's drunk. It's just the same as him being gone. Dex takes care of me. I need him."

She pulled her gaze away from the heaped cash and looked again at Canton's face. The temptation to snatch up the money and run fluttered away like a bird.

Oh, God, why do I have to pick now to start turning moral and upright? But I can't help it. I can't let anything bad happen to this poor man.

"Is something bad going to happen to Dex?" Canton asked. "Can you make him wake up, so he can get away? I've had dreams lately. A big shadow, coming after Dex. It gets him, and I'm all alone." He looked deeply at her, and lifted a hand to touch her face. "I'm sorry Dex hit you. I don't know why he did. Dex isn't bad most of the time. Most of the time he's good, and he takes care of me."

Her mind raced. She didn't have much more time. If she delayed her return much longer, Devil Jack would surely grow suspicious.

"Canton, there's a man in town. He's come after Dex, and he could be very dangerous to him. And to you. We need to talk, very quickly. Can I come in?"

He stared at her. His lip began to tremble, and tears spilled down his face. Nodding, he stepped aside and let her in, closing the door behind her.

Chapter Eleven

A few minutes later, Mary Alice McGee walked nervously across the street, trying to look as calm as possible, wondering what reaction she would receive when she reached Devil Jack. She wondered as well why she was so undecisive and pliable. One moment she was driven to see Dex Otie punished because of her earlier humiliation, the next, to keep him protected for the sake of his poor brother.

She crossed through the alley and came to the shed where Devil Jack Murchison waited for her.

"I'm here," she said into the darkness.

He emerged, a dark and looming form. "Well, where is he? Is he coming?"

"No," she said. "I'm sorry. He and his brother are already gone."

Devil Jack swore violently. "Gone! Where?"

"I don't know. The room was empty when I got there."

He swore some more and paced about. She saw in his threatening, brewing-storm manner how such a man might have earned the nickname of "Devil."

"I want to see for myself," he said. "With my own eyes. And if I find you've lied to me, I'll make you regret it."

"They're not there," she said. "I promise. Why would I lie to you?"

"What was the number of their room?"

"B1."

As Mary Alice watched from the shadows, Devil Jack Murchison crossed the street to the hotel and entered the empty lobby. Quietly he slipped up the stairs, seeking to make as little noise as possible.

On the second level he felt beneath his coat for one of the pistols he carried, and clamped his hand around the butt of it. He studied the numbers on the doors, and saw "B1" on the one closest by. He put his ear to its panel and listened. Nothing. Gently he touched the knob, and found it locked.

He rapped softly, unthreateningly. No reply from inside.

Still unpersuaded, he put pressure against the knob with his hand. It held, but he noticed it was rattly and loose. Somebody had forced this door open in the past, more than once, and the workings of it, several times repaired, were none too strong.

Glancing about to make sure no one was there to see him, he hammered his shoulder against the door once, twice, muffling the sound with his big body. On the third ram, the latch gave and the door swung open onto an empty room.

He stood there, filling the doorway, pistol in hand, staring into the vacant chamber. No clutter, no clothing tossed over the back of a chair, no saddlebags in the corner to indicate occupancy. Whoever had been in here last wasn't just momentarily away. They'd obviously checked out.

Slowly the pistol lowered, and Devil Jack Murchison shook his head and felt oddly like crying.

They really were gone. *With all that beautiful money.*

He turned and pulled the door closed behind him, but he'd ruined the latch and it wouldn't catch anymore.

Leaving the door ajar, tucking the pistol away under his coat, he turned back to the stairs . . . and heard a cough from behind one of the doors on down the hall.

He paused, wondering. *Maybe she had the wrong room. Maybe they're here, in some other room.*

He went to the door from behind which the cough had emerged, and put his ear close to it. Someone was moving about inside in a heavy, masculine manner.

Jack rapped on the door.

"Yeah? Who is it?"

"Pardon me, sir," he said, making his voice a little higher than its usual low grumble. "I've got a message for you."

"Message? What kind of message?"

"Telegram."

"Well, hold on a minute . . . let me get some pants on."

By the time the man swung open the door, Devil Jack had already deciphered that he wasn't Dex Otie. This was an older fellow, broader and bigger, with thick sideburns and a mustache that covered his entire mouth. He wore only his trousers, held up by one suspender hooked over a bare shoulder.

"Mr. Augustus Brodey?" Devil Jack said.

"Brodey? No, no. You've got the wrong place, mister."

"Oh. Well, I'm sorry to have bothered you. I was led to believe that Mr. Augustus Brodey was in this room.

Perhaps I have the wrong room number. Do you know who else is on this floor?''

''No, sir, I can't say I do.''

''Mr. Brodey, I believe, has a half-wit brother.''

The man narrowed his eyes. ''I don't believe I've seen nobody like that. But I only checked in this morning.''

''Oh. Well, thank you. I'll inquire with the hotel man downstairs.''

The man looked him over. ''Where's the telegram?''

''In my pocket.''

''Oh. Well, good evening.'' He closed the door.

Devil Jack moved down to another door, B4, and knocked there. No answer. He stuck his ear to the door and heard nothing, then peered through the keyhole. Black. Another empty room.

He moved over to B2, knocked, and listened again.

On the other side of the door, a terrified Canton Otie slipped his hand across his mouth in the darkness and struggled against the impulse to moan. He prayed that Dex, still passed out with his head on the table, would make no noise.

He knew who was out there and why he had come. Mary Alice McGee had warned him, and told him not to answer any knock, not even to make a sound.

Devil Jack Murchison listened hard through the door panel, then dropped to his knees and peered through the keyhole. Darkness, just like the prior room.

''Hell!'' he muttered, standing. ''How empty is this damn hotel?''

He moved down the hall to the stairs, a knot of hot anger rising in his gut.

Dexter Otie had gotten away. Murdered his brother, taken his money . . . and gotten away.

And Devil Jack had no idea how he'd ever be able to track him down.

*   *   *

Mary Alice was gone. He'd told her to wait for him, but she hadn't. Devil Jack looked around the shed and its surroundings, calling softly for her, but she was gone.

That was odd. She'd seemed awfully eager at the beginning to help him get Dex Otie. Downright enthusiastic, in fact. Then she'd come back talking about the room being empty, and now that he thought about it, with a manner that seemed subtly but certainly changed.

Something was afoot here. Something had happened between the time Mary Alice McGee went to that hotel and when she had come back.

He returned to the street and looked at the hotel again, studying the windows, figuring out which windows went with which rooms. The windows were dark. No unexplained movement of curtains and shifting of shadows presented themselves.

He turned away toward his own hotel, wondering if it was really over already and Dex had gotten away from him.

Mostly he wondered why Mary Alice had vanished so unexpectedly. Disappointed, angry, suspicious, and thinking very hard, he trod down the walk toward his lodging.

Mary Alice McGee slipped out of the shadows that hid her and watched Devil Jack Murchison stride away. When he was out of sight, she slinked quietly back to the Goodpasture Hotel.

This time she was almost caught by the clerk, who emerged from his office with his head buried in a newspaper just as she slipped around the landing. She darted up the stairs to room B2, where she lightly scratched the door with her fingernail. She'd told Canton earlier to keep the lights out and to respond to no knock or call—only to a scratch on the door.

Canton's nervous voice, sounding vaguely like that of

a ghost, emerged from the other side. "Is it you?"

"It's me," she said. "It's all right. You can let me in."

The door opened to her. She slipped in and closed the door behind her as her nose was assaulted by the stench of urine. Either Dex had wet himself in his drunken stupor at the table, or Canton had peed his pants in sheer fright while Devil Jack had been knocking on his door.

"He was here!" Canton said, his voice high. "He was here! He was here! He was here—"

"Hush, hush!" she said, reaching for him in the darkness, holding his shoulders. "I know he was here. Did he try to come in?"

"He knocked on the door. I was so scared, so scared, so scared—"

"But you kept quiet. You did good. I know you did. If you hadn't, he'd have come in on you."

Dex moaned at the table and moved. His head rose in the darkness.

"I did good?" Canton said.

"You did good. But the danger ain't over."

"Who the . . . where's the light, Canton? Canton, you here?" Dex tried to rise, but stumbled against the table. In the darkness Mary Alice felt something like falling leaves brush her leg.

He's knocked some of that money off the table! Temptation struck again quick and hard, and she yielded, ducking low and scooping up a handful of bills, which she quickly tucked down her bosom, an act unseen in the blackness.

"Dex, he was here! The man came *here,* and if I hadn't kept quiet and all, he'd have killed us, and—"

"Canton? Where's the light? Where's the damn lamp?" Dex stumbled again and bumped hard against Mary Alice. "Who the hell—"

"Hello, Sugarplum," she said. "Or Dex, I should say.

It's me, and if you ain't too drunk to understand me, I want to tell you that I saved your sorry life tonight.''

"Mary Alice . . . where am I?" He chuckled suddenly. "I'm drunk. I'm drunk as a redskin! Wah! Where's the lamp? Canton, light the lamp . . . let me count . . . my money . . .'' He lurched to the side and vomited abruptly. The smell of it mixed foully with the urine stench in the room, and Mary Alice wondered why she was doing this. But she knew why. For Canton. She couldn't let a man like Devil Jack harm an innocent like Canton.

"Don't light the lamp, Canton," she instructed. "He may be watching the hotel, and the light could give you away. Dex, are you sober enough to understand what I tell you?"

He muttered something vague.

"Listen to me. A man named Jack Murchison is in town, and he's looking for you."

Dex's voice sounded a trace clearer all at once. "Devil Jack . . . he's *here*?"

"The devil's chasing us, Dex!" Canton squealed. "The devil's chasing us, chasing us, chasing—"

"Shut up, boy! Shut up now!" Dex came to his feet and faced Mary Alice in the dark, grasping her shoulders. His breath stunk in her face. "How do you know? Where is he now?"

"I'll tell you everything I can, but first you have to get out of this room, out of this hotel," she said. "He came here looking for you earlier, but I was able to warn Canton to keep quiet and not answer, and to keep the light out so he'd think the room didn't have nobody in it. It worked . . . for now. But he's determined to find you. He claims you have money that's his. He claims you killed—"

"Hush!" Dex said, shaking her. His lips came close

to her ear, whispering. "Canton doesn't know! I don't want him to know."

"She said 'killed,' Dex," Canton said. "Why'd she say 'killed'?"

"Nothing you need to fret about," Dex replied. He gave Mary Alice another shake, but this one more gentle. "Listen, I'm sorry about how I done you back in the saloon. I was wrong to do it. I want you to forgive me. And to help me. I need to know about Devil Jack, anything you can tell me." The shock of her news had knocked some of the edge off his drunkenness, but his words were still slurred and he was unstable on his feet. "Damn, I wish I wasn't so drunk!" he said. "I wish I could clear out my head. . . ." He let go of her and turned, bumping the table again.

She felt another falling bill brush her foot, and in the darkness a change came, one that the brothers would not have seen even if the lamp had been burning. Mary Alice McGee, who had already this evening gone from would-be avenger to protector—for Canton's sake, certainly not Dex's—transformed yet again, becoming again the self-serving schemer that was her most familiar role. After all, she reasoned, she had already endangered herself for these men. Why not see what she could get out of it for herself?

"I'll tell you everything and do my best to help you— *if* you'll pay me sweet enough."

"Pay you . . ."

"I want a thousand dollars."

"A thousand . . . the hell!"

"Either that or I turn you over to Devil Jack." And at that Canton squealed and hunkered down in the dark room, cowering and childishly afraid, and she wished she hadn't said it.

Dex said, "Look, woman, I'm drunk, it's dark, and I don't know nothing about nothing that's going on here, nor whether Devil Jack's even really about this town. Seems to me like you're trying to pull something, trying to cut yourself in on a deal.''

"Suit yourself,'' she said, and made as if to leave.

"Don't go!'' Canton pleaded. "Please don't go get Devil Jack! Dex, don't let her go!''

Dex stepped forward, standing between her and the door. "Wait. You tell me something, woman. You swear it to God. Is Devil Jack really in this town?''

"He is. I swear to God. And he's after you because of . . . because of what he says happened.'' She paused. "Did it? What he said?''

Dex didn't reply, but she vaguely discerned his quick nod in the darkness.

"Then you'd best trust me. And you'd best pay me. I want my thousand dollars.''

Dex held silence a moment, then said, "All right. Damn it, all right! But not here. When we get to the livery. You're staying with us all the way there. If you're leading us into a trap, you're damn sure going to be right beside us when we walk into it.''

She didn't want to go with them. What if Devil Jack showed up and caught her betraying him? But on the other hand, she was sure she'd receive no money from Dex unless she was fully cooperative. "I'll go with you. There's no trap,'' she said. "Now you'd best gather up your things and get out of this hotel. And do it without a lamp. Is the curtain drawn?''

"Yes,'' Canton said. "It's drawed, it's drawed, it's drawed.''

"If you strike so much as a match, cup it in your hand to keep the light away from the window. I have a feeling he may watch this hotel tonight. He really wants you.''

"But how did he *know*?" Dex said. "I covered every track, every blasted clue . . ."

"You didn't. There was a letter, written by Devil Jack's brother. It told everything."

"A letter . . ."

"That's right. He wrote it and left it beside his bed. Devil Jack found it. Now you'd best get to moving. There's a window at the end of the hall, looking out onto the alley. It's the only safe way out, if he's watching. And don't forget my thousand."

"I won't forget." Dex sounded almost sober now. "Come on, Canton. Start to packing up everything. However you can, in whatever you can. Use the pillowcases. And for God's sake, don't stir that window curtain. He might be watching, and as far as he knows this is supposed to be an empty room."

Chapter Twelve

He was out there. She could feel it.

Out there, and wondering where she was and why she had betrayed him.

Mary Alice McGee moved in a swirl of intense and contrary emotions, knowing her time was short. At any moment he might appear at her door, in her room—and what would happen after that was a question she had no desire to answer.

Her dress lay in a heap on the floor, and she struggled almost wildly to get herself into an outfit of male clothing, left behind here in her room by a man who had been forced to flee in a most underdressed state when a couple of enemies interrupted him while he and she were intimately occuppied. He'd never returned to reclaim his garments.

She struggled into the trousers and tucked the tail of

114

the shirt into them. Too large, but the galluses would keep them up.

On the table against the wall lay a heap of bills. Five hundred dollars—only half the amount that she had demanded of Dex, but all that Dex had been willing to pay once they reached the livery. But it didn't matter. Canton, dear, innocent Canton, had made the difference. Having noted that Dex failed to pay her all he had promised, Canton had slipped to her a necklace he had dug out of one of the saddlebags without Dex noticing. He gave it to her almost childishly, like a boy giving a shiny stone to a girl he liked—and she had forced herself not to react to the fact that this was obviously a very valuable necklace. Diamond—she'd checked this already by scratching the stones against a glass. How much was this necklace worth? Her mouth went dry speculating about it.

She'd already hidden the necklace inside one of the slightly oversized boots that she would slip on to complete her male regalia. That necklace, along with the cash Dex had given her, would pave her path to a new and better life.

She glanced at the clock on her wall and mentally tried to calculate how far out of town Dex and Canton would have made it by now. They'd gotten out the hotel window without incident, and traveled a shadowed route to the livery and their horses, paying the liveryman quite generously to get the mounts out and saddled with all due speed, along with a promise to keep his mouth shut should anyone come asking after them. It was at that point that Dex had given her the five hundred and Canton had slipped her the necklace.

"Where you going from here?" she'd asked Canton.

"Dex says Denver," he'd replied.

"Denver. It's a good town. I may go there myself sometime. Maybe I'll see you."

"I hope so," Canton had replied, his smile bright as the diamond he'd slipped to her.

As she finished dressing, it came to mind that the necklace had certainly come from one of those poor corpses Dex had robbed on that fallen train. That bothered her a little bit . . . but not as much as her worry over how Dex might treat Canton after he discovered the necklace was missing. She hoped he wouldn't be too hard on him.

She slipped on the boots. The necklace, crammed into the toe, was a little uncomfortable, but also felt secure. She went to the table and swept up the money, stuffing it in one of the pockets. Topping herself off with a flop hat, she found it too large, but not a bad fit once her hair was tucked up inside.

Her dress and other feminine garb went into the old feed sack that served as her only piece of luggage. She was ready now.

After extinguishing the low-burning light and immersing the room in darkness, she went to the window and cautiously looked out onto the street, looking for Devil Jack Murchison. She did not see him. Quietly she raised the window, made a final scan of the street, and stepped onto the ledge. Pulling her bag through after her, she edged along the ledge and around the corner and out of the street—just in time to see Devil Jack Murchison appear on the far side, crossing toward the saloon.

She'd be willing to bet he wasn't coming for a drink. She could guess what had gone on: He'd been thinking things over in his room, and was coming to ask questions she didn't want to answer. Maybe coming to do worse than that.

Hurrying, she crossed to the other roof and down to the rear alley. Her heart pounded almost audibly and she felt light-headed with fear.

The black fellow at the livery looked at her oddly when she arrived, frowning into her face.

"I need a way out of town, fast," she said. "I'll pay you for a wagon ride to the Lodgetree Station." She dug in her pocket and brought out money. "Here. Take it. Get me away from here as fast as you can."

He squinted at her while he took the bills. "You're a woman."

"Yes."

"And you was here earlier. With them two men. And you weren't dressed that way."

"No. And there'll be no more questions, and no more answers. Do you have a wagon you can hitch fast?"

"No wagon. But I got a fast horse, and you can ride double behind me. You care if folks see you?"

"I do care. I don't want to be seen."

"Then you won't be. I know ways to go there ain't nobody going to see."

"Then take me. As fast as you can. And if anyone comes asking—"

"I know. Don't say a word. Just like before, with them two men."

"That's right. How fast can you saddle that fast horse?"

"Just watch me, ma'am . . . or sir. Just watch me."

Lodgetree Station, Colorado

She was back in her feminine garb again, but her hair was a travesty, ruined by too long a confinement inside that man's hat.

Mary Alice McGee had little experience as a rider, and the jolting nocturnal run out of Goodpasture while clinging to the back of the liveryman had left her sore and trembling. But there were no regrets. The liveryman had done what he promised, keeping them out of sight and moving swiftly. The farther they had gone, the safer she had felt. Devil Jack Murchison might figure out her betrayal, but he would never find her now—she hoped.

Lodgetree Station was little more than its name implied: a mountain whistle-stop with a few cabins and houses about, one general store, and a decrepit railroad hotel with a small café in one corner of its lower level. Despite its proximity to Goodpasture, Mary Alice had never before been to Lodgetree, and had no desire to remain now. But what she had just been told by the man behind the train station counter made it seem likely she'd have a chance to get to know the little community, like it or not.

"Tomorrow morning?" she asked again, as if asking could make a difference. "You're sure?"

"Yes, ma'am, of course I'm sure," the man replied. "It's my job to know the schedules, and I'm telling you there's no other Denver-bound trains that will be stopping here until tomorrow morning."

"No others."

"That's right, ma'am. That's what I told you."

She looked around unhappily. "One hotel? That's all there is here?"

"We're a small place, ma'am."

"Well . . . I suppose it'll have to do. And that I'll have to wait until tomorrow morning."

"If you want to catch a train to Denver at this station, yes, ma'am, you will have to wait," he said wearily. "You want to go ahead and buy a ticket now?"

"Yes. Yes, I do."

"All righty. Return ticket too?"

For the first time, she smiled at him. "No. No return. I'm not coming back."

They made the transaction. "Anything else I can do for you, ma'am?"

"No, thank you," she said, picking up her bag and walking toward the squalid hotel.

The man at the desk might have been a brother to the fellow at the train station. Same aged face, same receded and whitish hairline, same weary attitude. He rented her a room with hardly a word, and she made her way up the narrow flight of stairs, wondering if Denver-bound trains ever came chugging along outside the official schedule. She supposed not.

The room was cramped, drab, ugly, the bed sagging and draped in wrinkled bedclothes that looked as if they had needed a washing maybe a week ago and were still waiting. She didn't care. Tossing down the bag, she flopped back on the bed and stared at the ceiling.

She wished Lodgetree were a little farther away from Goodpasture than it was. What if Devil Jack came?

But he won't come, she counseled herself. It wasn't her he was after, but Dex Otie. He might be angry with her, suspecting she had betrayed him, might even be dangerous to her if they happened to meet, but it didn't seem likely he'd actually come after her. What good would that do him, after all?

Unless, she thought, he figured she could lead him to wherever Dex Otie had gone.

Denver. Canton had told her. Now she wished he hadn't.

She went to the bedroom door and locked it, or tried. The latch wouldn't catch. So instead she scooted a chair against the knob and tried to pin the door shut that way, vowing not to leave this room until it was time to catch that train come morning.

She brought out the necklace and studied it, watching the light catch and refract through the gleaming diamond. Beautiful. The most beautiful sight she had ever seen. She hid the diamond in the boot again and fetched out the bills, laying them on the table and admiring them, too. She'd never felt so wealthy as she did right now. Nor so full of hope. She was really going to get away, really escape, find some place where she could be a real woman, a real human being, not just a piece of feminine flesh to be used by strangers in a little room above a Colorado mining-town saloon.

Her sleepless night had left her exhausted, and soon she was asleep on her bed, still fully clothed. Hours passed without her knowledge, and when she opened her eyes again, the sun was edging toward the western horizon.

And Devil Jack Murchison was standing beside her bed, looking down at her.

"I'm surprised at you," he said. "Did you think I couldn't figure where you'd go?"

She sat up, blinking. "Is this real . . . or am I dreaming?"

"This is real."

"Don't hurt me."

"Don't hurt you." He chuckled. "Don't hurt you, you say. You betrayed me, woman. You said you'd help me get my hands on Dex Otie. You seemed downright eager to help me, matter of fact. Then you betrayed me. Helped him and his brother get away."

"No. It ain't true. I swear!"

He flicked his glance toward the table and the money that lay there.

"That'd be mine. Some of the same money that my brother was bringing in to divide with me before everything went . . . bad. How much?"

"Five hundred dollars."

"Most of it still there?"

"Yes."

"I know you spent thirty of it, paying off that nigger at the livery." He reached in a pocket and brought out just that amount. He tossed it on the bed. "Talkative darky, that one was, once I persuaded him. Told me everything—you and Dex and the half-wit, and then you coming along later dressed up like a man, asking to come to Lodgetree. He sang it all out to me. Only mistake he made was trying to resist me at the beginning. It would have gone a hell of a lot easier for him if he hadn't.''

"Don't hurt me," she asked again.

He took a step toward her. "Maybe I won't, if you'll talk. If you'll tell me where Dex Otie has gone."

"Please . . . I don't know."

"I'd say you know. I'd say you know a lot. Why you want to protect him, woman? Didn't you tell me he slapped you down before a whole saloonful of men?" He was leaning toward her now, hand reaching out.

"I . . . I don't care about him. You can have him, kill him, do anything you want to him. It's his brother I wanted to protect."

"The dummy?" He laughed; his hand touched her arm now and clawed around it. "Why do you care for a *dummy*?"

"Please, please don't hurt me! Please!"

"It doesn't have to go all that hard for you. Just talk, and I'll be . . . well, I can't say as how I'll be nice, but I won't make it so hard on you as otherwise. Now talk to me, woman. Tell me where Dex Otie and his brother are going. Tell me now."

Part III
The Betrayer

Chapter Thirteen

Denver, Colorado

He awakened with a grunt upon the first rattling of his door, was on his feet when the first knock came, and was cowering behind the bed with a pistol in hand when the knocking finished. He was clad only in long underwear, the back flap down and flopping, and his reddish hair, uncombed for days, stuck up like thatch.

Lippy Blake was good at cowering. He'd been at it for years, starting back in Madison County, North Carolina, where he'd cowered away the entire Civil War, somehow managing to avoid the rebel conscription that had taken his friends—all three of them—to the front lines and bloody deaths. Since moving to Colorado, he'd done most of his cowering to avoid the creditors who financed his occasional plunges into gambling.

"Who's there?" he bellowed, if a nearly soprano voice could truly be said to bellow.

"Lippy? Is that you? Are we at the right place?"

"Listen here—you tell Mr. Lee I'll have his money to him quick as I can!" Lippy called back. "Next Tuesday at the latest—I swear!"

"What are you talking about, Lippy?"

Lippy stood, frowning, and after a few moments' consideration, came out from behind the bed. "Who you be out there?"

"Don't you recognize the sound of your own kin, Lippy?"

Lippy laid the pistol aside and went to the door. "Is this who I think it is?"

"It's likely."

Lippy opened the door and looked out on the faces of Dex and Canton Otie. Dex had a smug look; Canton was grinning like a child.

"I be. It is you."

"You don't sound too happy to see us, Lippy," Dex said.

"Why you here?"

"We've come to be boarders. Keep you a bit of company for a time. Canton and me are laying low just now."

Lippy chuckled without a trace of mirth and started to close the door. Dex put a foot out and blocked it.

"Now, Lippy, you ain't being nice. Didn't I tell you we was coming as *boarders,* not visitors?"

"What do you mean?"

Dex held up a handful of bills. Lippy's mud-colored eyes grew wide, his tongue thrashing out over the thick lips that had given him his nickname.

"Visitors stay free. Boarders pay."

Lippy licked his lips again and stepped back. "Come in, cousins, come in! I been wanting to visit with you boys for the longest time now! Come in and set!"

*　　*　　*

"What's the matter with you, Lippy?" Dex asked as Lippy gazed limpidly at the pile of bills Dex had laid out on the dirty tabletop. He'd not laid out nearly all the money he had—he knew Lippy well enough to know how foolish that would be—but he'd put out enough to make an impression. He wanted Lippy to know he had money, but not exactly how much. An element of mystery, combined with some modest passing of a few "rent" dollars every now and then, would tend to keep Lippy quiet and content to let them reside there for a time, in that low-profile section of town, inhabited by low-profile humanity. Keeping a low profile was important to Dex just now.

"It's beautiful," Lippy said. "Mighty beautiful. You ever see anything prettier than money?"

"You're right, Lippy. It is beautiful. And I got more than what you see there. Already safe in a big old vault at the bank downtown."

Lippy asked, "Just how much money you got?"

"Enough."

"What you going to do with it?"

"Turn it into even more."

Lippy looked as if he might cry; his face was like that of a sensitive soul being stirred by a magnificent and emotional symphony. "Even more," he repeated. "Even more. How you going to do it?"

Dex grinned and mimed the act of shuffling a deck of cards. Lippy suddenly looked solemn. "A man can lose as much as win in the gaming halls. I know."

"My luck's always been good in Denver."

Lippy leaned closer. "How'd you get the money, Dex?"

"Never you mind."

Lippy chuckled. "So I figured. So I figured." His caterpillarlike brows crawled a quarter-inch closer together. "Ain't nobody after this money, is there?"

Dex felt Canton's glance, ignored it. "No." And he edged his foot beneath the table and touched Canton's ankle, just to send the message: *Keep your mouth shut.*

"Come on, Dex, tell me how you got it!"

"No need for you to know. I got it. That's what matters."

"Did you rob a bank?"

"I ain't talking, Lippy."

"Dex, it's eating me up, not knowing!"

"Speaking of eating, where's breakfast?"

"I ain't fixed it yet. I'll fix it now if you'll tell me where you got the money."

"How about this—you fix the breakfast, and I *don't* tell you where I got it."

Lippy was as bad a cook as he was a housekeeper, but hunger is the best of spices and made up for what the food lacked. After they had eaten, Dex brought out cigars for himself and Lippy, and a bit of bittersweet chocolate for Canton. He'd bought it back in Goodpasture, on the sneak, to give his brother as a surprise. Canton accepted the candy enthusiastically, ripped it out of the paper wrapper, and crammed most of it into his mouth in one bite.

"Where can a man go to buy himself some good clothes around here?" Dex asked around the butt of his cigar.

"Good clothes? Fancy duds, you mean?"

"That's right. A man plans to do some high-stakes gambling, he needs to look the part."

"I ain't never had fancy duds. I wear castoffs most the time."

"I'll find a good clothes shop on my own, then."

"You going to buy me some clothes, too?" Canton asked.

"You don't need no more clothes," Dex replied. "Lippy, you got any more coffee?"

GET YOUR 4 FREE BOOKS NOW—
A VALUE BETWEEN $16 AND $20

Mail the Free Book Certificate Today!

FREE BOOKS CERTIFICATE!

YES! I want to subscribe to the Leisure Western Book Club. Please send my 4 FREE BOOKS. Then, each month, I'll receive the four newest Leisure Western Selections to preview FREE for 10 days. If I decide to keep them, I will pay the Special Members Only discounted price of just $3.36 each, a total of $13.44. This saves me between $3 and $6 off the bookstore price. There are no shipping, handling or other charges. There is no minimum number of books I must buy and I may cancel the program at any time. In any case, the 4 FREE BOOKS are mine to keep—at a value of between $17 and $20! Offer valid only in the USA.

Name_____

Address_____

City_____ State_____

Zip_____ Phone_____

Biggest Savings Offer!

For those of you who would like to pay us in advance by check or credit card—we've got an even bigger savings in mind. Interested? Check here. ☐

If under 18, parent or guardian must sign.
Terms, prices and conditions subject to change. Subscription subject to acceptance. Leisure Books reserves the right to reject any order or cancel any subscription.

GET FOUR BOOKS TOTALLY *FREE*—A VALUE BETWEEN $16 AND $20

PLEASE RUSH
MY FOUR FREE
BOOKS TO ME
RIGHT AWAY!

Leisure Western Book Club
P.O. Box 6613
Edison, NJ 08818-6613

AFFIX
STAMP
HERE

"Plumb out."

Dex flipped out a bill. "Why don't you run buy us some more, then."

Lippy grabbed the bill, rose, and scurried away like an eager rodent.

"Lippy."

The little man spun and waited. "Yeah?"

"Keep what's left over."

Lippy grinned and nodded, and hurried out the door.

Dex smiled and puffed his cigar. This wasn't much of a castle, but here, for a time, he knew he could be king, and Lippy his loyal subject.

They'd gotten away from Goodpasture and Devil Jack Murchison. The money was still theirs, and in the gambling halls he was sure he could make it multiply.

This could turn out to be a lot of fun.

Dex bought his clothes later in the day, and that night headed into Denver with cash in his pockets and his heart in his throat. Denver had always been a lucky city for him, and he'd made money here before in its seamier, seedier gambling dives. . . . But this was different. Bigger dollars, bigger stakes, bigger losses, if losses came.

But a potential for bigger wins, too.

Well past midnight, Dex Otie, still spiffed up in his new finery and still smelling of the scented water splashed on him earlier in the day by the barber who had trimmed his hair and shaved his beard, rode a horse-drawn cab back toward the little city-limits hovel of Lippy Blake. He paid and tipped the cabby, generously, and strode broadly toward the house.

Lippy was still up, waiting on him.

"How was the luck?"

Dex loosened his collar, grinned, and flopped back

into a chair. "Good," he said. "The luck was good. Real good."

Lippy smiled broadly. "I'm glad for you, Dex."

"The hell! You're glad for yourself. You know that as long as I'm making good money, you'll get plenty of boarder rent."

"I can't fool you, can I!" Lippy maintained his grin, but his manner became subtly more serious. "Dex, I want you to tell me something. If you've got the money to dress all fine and gamble in the big halls, why are you holing up in a ditch like this place?"

"Just laying low, Lippy. Reasons of my own."

"Dex, is there somebody after you?"

Dex paused, then said, "Not no more."

"Then why are you hiding?"

"Lippy, you ask too many questions. You keep that up and you might just talk me into looking for a different landlord to pay my money to."

Lippy blinked and chuckled uncertainly. "I just want to know if that money's really your money."

"Since when did you turn honest?"

"It ain't honesty. It's knowing that stole money draws trouble . . . and any trouble that money draws, it'll draw here."

"Don't worry about it, Lippy. There'll be no trouble."

Lippy rose. "I hope not. Well, g'night. I'm tired. I'm going to bed."

"Go ahead. I'm going to set up awhile and count my winnings."

Lippy departed toward the rear room, and Dex began his count. Lippy watched him, silently, from the darkness, but Dex knew he was there, staring at the money, licking those big lips like a very hungry little man.

* * *

Dex went into town the next morning without explanation, and Lippy grew worried, the talk about a new landlord not forgotten. He'd taken it as banter . . . but what if Dex had meant it, and had gone looking?

Canton had slept later than the others, and was still at his breakfast when Dex left. Lippy, at the moment unemployed, hadn't had a cent come in for days, until Dex had shown up and given him a generous payment for a month's lodging. Dex and Canton, almost forgotten relatives a week before, were now very important to him, keys to the only possible success he could foresee. So Lippy went to the table and pulled up near Canton, pasting a wide grin on his face.

"Them eggs good, Canton?"

"Yes."

"You want some more?"

Canton smacked his lips and chewed in a way that revealed visions to disgust a lesser man than Lippy Blake. "No. I got plenty."

"You want more later on, you just tell me. I want you and Dex to be happy here. I want you to stay."

"Thank you, Lippy."

"You know what, Canton? I like you. I like you because you're the kind of man what tells the truth, and don't hold nothing back."

Canton took another bite and waited for Lippy to go on.

"In fact, Canton, I'm counting on you to be truthful with me right now. I want you to tell me if somebody's after Dex. Because of that money, you know."

"I ain't supposed to talk about nothing like that. Dex says."

"That right? Well . . . he wouldn't have said that if there wasn't somebody after him, it don't seem to me."

Canton, not following that, scooped up a biscuit and another bite of eggs.

Lippy got a cunning look; a lie spilled off his heavy lips with practiced ease. "Canton, I don't want to scare you or nothing, but there was somebody who come asking for Dex last night. After you'd gone to sleep, but before Dex got back. Looking for Dex, this person was."

Canton stopped chewing and stared at Lippy.

"Asking about Dex, yep. But I wouldn't say nothing. No, sir. Not me."

"Who was it?" Canton asked. His voice was different now.

"Well, I don't know. Who do you think it might be?"

"It wasn't . . . it wasn't that Devil Jack Murchison, was it?"

Lippy jerked back, the cunning look replaced by one of cold shock. "Devil Jack . . . you telling me that Devil Jack is after Dex?"

"I can't tell you nothing. Dex said not to tell nothing."

"What the hell would Dex have done to get Devil Jack after him?"

"You know Devil Jack?"

"I know him. Sweet Christmas! Is that Devil Jack's money that Dex has?"

Canton was beginning to look very disturbed, moving toward an emotional outburst. "I don't know . . . Devil Jack was here? He was *here*?"

Lippy shook his head. "No, no. It wasn't Devil Jack. It was . . . You know, I don't think it was anybody. I think maybe I just fell asleep and dreamed that. Yep. That's it. I dreamed that somebody came asking. That's all."

Canton swallowed hard. "You sure, Lippy?"

"Yeah. Yeah. I'm sure now."

"I didn't say nothing about Devil Jack, Lippy. I didn't say that he's chasing Dex and me."

"No, you didn't."

"Don't tell Dex I said nothing like that, 'cause I didn't."

"I know. I won't tell."

Canton got up from the table and left the rest of his breakfast untouched. Lippy, watching him, reached over and began eating the remnants with his fingers.

So Dex's money was really Devil Jack's.

No wonder Dex was avoiding hotels. Devil Jack wasn't a man one messed around with. *If it was me,* Lippy thought, *I'd not even be showing myself in the saloons. No, sir! Not with Devil Jack on my tail.*

Chapter Fourteen

Some days later, Lippy Blake sat in a run-down Denver saloon, sipping beer he'd paid for with money stolen from Canton's pocket. He was deeply lost in thought, deeply worried.

Had been, in fact, since he'd picked up that business about Devil Jack Murchison from Canton. Devil Jack! Not the kind of man you wanted to be on the bad side of. And Dex surely was, if that wealth of his was actually Devil Jack's.

Lippy recalled the time he'd seen and gained his respect for Devil Jack. Some years before the man had come through Denver with his brother, Wade; the pair of them had dropped into this very saloon. Lippy and Devil Jack—that's how the man had introduced himself—had somehow fallen into conversation together and gotten on quite well. Shared a few drinks, Devil Jack paying.

Then a drunk had come in, somebody the Murchison

brothers apparently knew and didn't much like. This was one of those blubbery, friendly drunks, and apparently also an ignorant one, because as he shoulder-slapped and slobbered over his "good old friend Devil Jack," he was the only man in the place who couldn't see that his "good old friend" didn't share the same feelings toward him, and was growing mighty weary of his company, fast. When the drunk had made a few comments about a certain woman—Lippy never really had caught on who she was, but figured she must have been some old lover of Devil Jack's—Devil Jack had roared, stood, picked the fellow up like a sack of dirt, and carried him, above his head, out the door. Lippy and most of the other saloon patrons followed.

What happened in the alley beside the saloon was ugly indeed, involving fists, kicks, several meetings of kneecap and groin, and even a touch of ornamental knifework that left the drunk with a slitted nose and a hacked-up left ear. Devil Jack had ended it all up by dumping the half-conscious man head-down in a cistern, laughing, cracking jokes about it, leaving the man to drown. Some other less hardened fellow had pulled the victim out. Somehow the battered man managed to get to his feet and stagger away. Nobody ever saw him again, though the town drunks swore that the skeletal remains of him had been found a few months later in an abandoned outhouse north of the city. He'd crawled in there and died from his beating, best anyone could guess. It couldn't be proved, of course, and nobody had bothered to inform the law about it anyway. He'd just been a stranger and a drunk, after all. Nobody who mattered.

Lippy sipped his beer and worried. Devil Jack was a good man to have liking you, but you didn't want to annoy him. And annoyed he'd surely be if he found somebody harboring a man who'd stolen from him.

Quite a predicament, this one. At the heart of it all was the money.

In one way, Lippy didn't much care whether the money was Devil Jack's, Dex's, or anybody else's. The point was to make it, or as much as possible of it, *his,* and to do it without getting killed.

He stared across the room, watching some men playing cards, and mulled the matter of Dexter Otie. That first couple of nights, Dex had done well at the gambling houses. He'd won substantial money. Then the third night he only broke even, and after that, lost. Not much, just a little . . . but the point was he'd come back with less than he'd taken with him. It was the same the night after that, too. And the next, except this time the losses were bigger.

If this kept up, Dex might run clear through every bit of that money. The thought made Lippy feel sick.

Even if Dex's luck changed and he started winning again, it didn't look as if this was going to do much for Lippy Blake. Dex had tossed him a few dollars in ''rent,'' but not all that much, and in the times Dex was away from the house, Lippy had managed to learn from Canton that Dex had far more cash available than he was ever letting Lippy see. And apparently some jewels and such, too. How Dex had stumbled upon such a haul was, however, a question still unanswered.

And how in particular had he come to get hold of Devil Jack's money? Another big question. But the biggest of all was, what was going to happen when Devil Jack finally tracked Dex Otie down? And who besides Dex was going to end up hurt or dead?

By plying Canton at every opportunity, Lippy had managed to settle in his own mind the fact that, yes, Devil Jack really was pursuing Dex. Or, at least, had been. Canton told vague and hard-to-follow tales of hiding in a hotel room in Goodpasture, some dream about a man-eating shadow, of cowering in the dark while Devil Jack himself pounded the door, of slipping out a window in the night and making a mad dash away from town, and ultimately to Denver. There was something about a "nice lady" somewhere in there, though Lippy never figured out just where she fit in.

The significant fact Canton had told him, however—probably repeating assurances Dex gave him in private—was that Devil Jack had been evaded. They'd escaped him, and there was no way he'd ever track them down.

Lippy wondered. If all that money was Devil Jack's, it seemed to him that Devil Jack would find a way to track it down. As for Dex's "laying low," as he always put it, what good was that when he was displaying himself in the gambling halls of Denver every night? How long would it take Devil Jack to come around to the notion that Denver might be just the kind of place a Colorado man with money might be drawn to?

Lippy lifted his glass and drained it, and through the murky bottom of it found the answer to his last question.

He lowered the glass slowly, staring, his wet, wide lips hanging open.

Standing in the doorway of the saloon was Devil Jack Murchison himself.

Lippy was up and out the back in an instant. He darted straight for the outhouse and closed himself in.

"Got to think, Lippy! You got to think!" He whispered it over and over, pounding his head with the heel of his right hand. "Think, Lippy, think!"

A minute or so later, when the shock and panic had subsided a little, he did think.

"All right, Lippy, here's how it is . . . the thing is not to lose that money, and not to get killed or nothing by Devil Jack . . . now, there's different things you could do . . . you could go tell Dex that Devil Jack is in town

. . . maybe he'd give you money to reward you . . . no, no, he wouldn't do that, not Dex . . . he'd just up and leave town, taking all the money with him . . . so maybe you could just keep mum, let whatever happens happen . . . maybe Devil Jack will just go off and not ever find Dex . . . but then Dex'll just keep gambling and losing, and sooner or later that money will be gone and you'll not have none of it for your own . . . so maybe what I should do is . . .''

He stopped, astonished at the conclusion to which his mental ramblings had led him. Could he really do what he was thinking of? What would the consequences be for Dex and Canton? Terrible, no doubt . . . but for Lippy himself, the consequences would surely be far better. At the very least, they'd take away from Devil Jack any incentive to hurt Lippy Blake.

He took a deep breath and nodded. ''All right, Lippy. That's what you got to do. Now, go and do it.''

He left the privy and entered the saloon through the rear door, looking around for Devil Jack and hoping he'd remember him from the time they'd drunk together that prior time.

But Lippy was given no chance to find out. Devil Jack was already gone.

Another breakfast, another chance to watch Canton chew with his mouth open.

Dex, meanwhile, picked at his food, looking very tired and sullen.

''How was the luck last night?'' Lippy asked, trying to sound nonchalant. Dex was touchy about that question at times.

Today, however, he merely sounded defeated. ''Luck was bad. Bad as hell. I lost . . . never mind how much I lost.''

Lippy tried not to show his worry. He forked some scrambled egg into his mouth. Canton, meanwhile, ate too, chewing far too vigorously.

"I don't believe I can keep it up," Dex went on. Lippy put down his fork. This was something new; Dex normally volunteered little about his gambling life.

"Whatcha mean, Dex?"

"I mean this gambling. I figured I'd come here and make that money turn into more money. I'd always had a lot of luck in Denver. But the luck's running out. I keep on gambling, I might just lose all I got."

"So whatcha wanting to do?"

"Quit gambling. Maybe even use that money to . . . I don't know, open me up a little business somewhere."

Lippy was beginning to feel queasy. "A little business."

"Yes."

"Where?"

"I don't know. Anywhere. Texas, Arkansas, Kansas . . ."

"What do you know about business?"

"Not much. But what I'm beginning to learn about gambling I don't much like. I'm learning that it's a sure-as-hell way to go broke fast."

"You can go broke in business, too."

"I reckon."

Canton was just now catching on. "We going to open a store, Dex?"

"I don't know what we'll do."

"I want a store. I want to sell candy and such."

"Hush up, Canton. Just eat."

Lippy said, "Dex, don't you be going and doing something foolish. You don't know nothing about running no business."

"What's it to you? It's my money."

No, it's Devil Jack's money, Lippy thought. *But if you*

go running off and sinking it into some business, it's gone money, and I'll never have a chance to get no good part of it at all. "I just think you ought to be careful."

"And keep gambling? Is that being careful?"

Lippy opened his mouth, then closed it. Nothing to say.

Lippy stood. "I got to get out a bit today," he announced.

"Where you going?" Canton asked.

"Just a few errands, that's all." He left before there was time for more questions . . .

. . . and set out to find Devil Jack Murchison, as quickly as he could.

It was dusk before he found him. He'd looked hard all day, asking questions, looking into bars, cafés, hotel lobbies. No Devil Jack had turned up.

He found him, ironically, only after he quit trying. He wandered listlessly into one of the same dives he'd poked his head into earlier in the day, and there he was, seated at a table in the rear, eating a plateful of beef and potatoes, drinking coffee.

Lippy stood staring as if he expected Devil Jack to vanish like a phantom. Jack turned his head slowly, and his eyes met Lippy's and narrowed.

Lippy wasn't smart, but he knew when a grin was called for. He flashed the most disarming one he could, nodded like a bow-and-scrape house servant, and came forward, taking off his hat as he did.

"I know you," Devil Jack said.

"Yes, sir, Mr. Murchison . . . Devil Jack. You do. Some years ago, we had a drink or two together right here in Denver."

"Yeah. Yeah. I remember now. I remember that night. It was a good night."

"A good night," he said. A good night because he

had the fun of beating a drunk so bad he crawled off and died. Lippy didn't dare allow the darkness of that thought to darken his smile.

"My name's Lippy. You remember?"

"I didn't. I do now. Good to see you, Lippy."

"I'd like to . . . sit down here if I could. Talk to you."

Jack's expression wasn't inviting. "Why?"

"I got something to tell you. Something I believe you'd like to hear."

"There's only one thing I'm wanting to hear these days, and I doubt there's a damn thing you'd know about it." He took a bite of meat and began to chew, the conversation over as far as he was concerned.

"I believe, sir, that it's the very thing I *do* know about."

Devil Jack stopped chewing and looked at him with suspicious curiosity.

"Dexter Otie," Lippy said.

Devil Jack lifted a big leg beneath the table and scooted out the chair opposite him. "Have a seat, Lippy," he said. "And start talking."

Lippy was back at his house long before Dex came in that night. Despite his growing doubts about the wisdom of gambling, Dex had been back at it tonight, trying one more time. Failing one more time.

Luck had deserted him. He was going to have to find another way. This wasn't working, and it just didn't *feel* right anymore.

Another thing didn't feel right, either. But he couldn't quite nail it down. The atmosphere had changed. Something to do with Lippy. Something subtle, but unnerving. Lippy was looking at him in awfully odd ways these days, that cunning little rat mind of his churning away at something behind those muddy eyes.

Dex was finding the notion of getting away from here

and coming up with some other way to seek his fortune to be increasingly attractive.

As he strode toward Lippy's house—he couldn't afford a hansom cab tonight, after all he'd lost—his mind drifted back to an incident that had happened in the gambling hall earlier in the evening. Nothing particularly significant, but it had stuck with him for some reason.

Two men had come into the gambling hall that night, and every eye in the place had turned toward them. Swarthy, dark of hair and eye, they had a manner about them that hinted of danger and strength, and it was evident they were fully aware of, and enjoying, the reaction they generated.

"Who are they?" Dex had asked a gambling partner.

"Killers. Killers for hire. Give them two a dollar and they'll bring you back a corpse."

Dex had immediately thought of Devil Jack Murchison. If he knew where the man could be found, he'd half consider hiring those two to take care of him, just to make sure he never managed to track him down, or encountered him by chance.

Just an idle fantasy, of course. With any luck, Devil Jack wouldn't find him at all, ever.

"With any luck." An ironic choice of phrase, Dex noted as his thoughts returned to the present. If his gambling results of late were an indication, luck was one thing he didn't have too much of just now.

He hurried across the yard to the door, the night suddenly feeling close and oppressive. He was eager to get inside.

Chapter Fifteen

Lippy was gone by breakfast the next morning. No message, no note. Could Lippy even write? Dex wasn't sure. In any case, all he left was an empty bed and chair.

Canton, meanwhile, was restless. "I'm tired of being here, Dex," he said. "All I do is stay here with Lippy. I walk around the yard, and up and down the street . . . but I get tired of it."

"I know," Dex said. "I'm tired of it too. Don't worry. We ain't staying much longer. I got some plans."

"I'm glad. I don't like it here. I been having them dreams again, Dex."

"The shadow that eats me up?"

"Yes."

"Boy, that ain't nothing, like I told you. Just a dream. There's no real shadow. There ain't nothing after us."

"There's Devil Jack."

"Devil Jack is gone. He doesn't know where we are.

143

When we left Goodpasture, nobody knew where we were going.''

Canton paused. "The lady did.''

"What?''

"The nice lady. Mary Alice. She knew we were coming to Denver.''

"How the hell did she know that? Canton, did you tell her?''

"I didn't think it would matter.''

Dex swore and shook his head. "Of all the . . .'' He rose from his breakfast chair and paced around a bit, rubbing his jaw, muttering. "Well . . . I don't reckon it matters. Unless she told Devil Jack, and I don't believe she would. She seemed to be truly trying to help us out.''

"I'm sorry, Dex.''

"Forget about it. We're leaving Denver tomorrow, anyhow.''

"We are?''

"That's right. No more of you having to sit around, staring at Lippy. We'll find us a better place, a place of our own. We'll give ourselves a new last name. I'll take our money and put it into a business. We'll settle down. See how we like it. And if we don't like it, well, hell, we can always sell out and take off again. Can't we!''

"That's right, Dex. That's right.'' Canton smiled broadly, his face, pallid since they had come to the city, filled again with color. He bounded boyishly from his chair. "We're leaving tomorrow?''

"Yep.''

"Why not today?''

"Because I'm feeling lucky today. I want one more chance at the gambling house. Just one more. I'll make back everything I've lost, then we'll say fare-thee-well to old Lippy and hit the road to . . . well, I don't even know. Some good place.''

"Let's leave today, Dex! Today!"

"Tomorrow morning, boy. That's soon enough. You can handle Lippy one more day, can't you?"

"Yes. I guess I can."

"Good boy." Dex looked around. "I wonder where he is, anyhow?"

Dex was drunk when he came back to Lippy's house that night. Luck hadn't smiled. He'd lost even more, until at last he stopped short, pulled himself away from the faro and keno and poker tables, and swore there'd be no more of it. The few dollars he had left went to liquor, Dex toasting his anticipated farewell to Denver again and again, until he was hardly able to stand.

The house was dark. Unusual. Lippy had some kind of light burning almost all the time. Of course, Lippy had not shown up even by the time Dex had left the house in the afternoon.

Something must be wrong.

He went to the door and found it not only unlocked but slightly ajar. There was no light inside.

"Canton?"

No answer.

"Boy? You in here?"

Silence.

Dex, wishing he wasn't so drunk, pushed the door open farther and went in, feeling his way along until he reached the table. He fumbled for matches, lit the wick.

There were papers on the center of the table, pinned there with a knife. Dex rubbed his red eyes, focused his vision by force of will. Pulling the knife from the table, he picked up the papers, dropped to his knees, held them close to the lamp. Read.

No. No!

He shook his head, trying to clear it, and read again. He laid the papers back on the table and came to his feet. Pulling up a chair, he sat down and stared into the flame of the wick, watching the oily black smoke from it rise out of the bowl and up to the dirty ceiling. He read the papers one more time, then held them above the bowl. They browned, smoked, broke into flame. He dropped them, watched them burn to ash.

"No," he whispered. "Not your way, Lippy. Not your way, Devil Jack. *My* way. My way."

Two hours later, in a seedy saloon on a dark street, a much more sober Dex Otie sat in a corner, waiting. Though his mind raced, his stomach burned as if he'd swallowed hot coals, and his heart felt like a fluttering bird beneath his ribs, Dex's exterior was calm, icily cool.

The light shifted; shadows moved across his table. He looked up into the dark faces of the two men who had drawn such attention upon their entrance into the gambling hall the day before.

"We hear you been asking to see us."

"I have. Sit down, gentlemen."

"Any particular reason we should?"

"There is. I hear you men can be . . . employed. Hired."

"For the right kind of work, we can." The accents were mildly Mexican, though the look hinted at a mix of bloodlines. "I've got the right kind of work in mind."

"Then the question now, amigo, is whether you can show the right kind of money."

Dex reached into his pocket and pulled out an impressive stack of bills. He plopped it on the tabletop, let them study it.

"Sit down, gentlemen," he invited again.

They sat.

Lippy Blake scooted a little farther down in his chair, trying to keep it balanced. If it tilted even an inch or two more to the left, he knew it would fall right off the back of the buffalo upon which it sat. If only the blasted buffalo would slow down . . . or at least run on the level floor instead of up and down this endless staircase . . .

He jerked suddenly, almost falling out of his chair. His eyes popped open as the bizarre dream vanished. The buffalo and the staircase and such gave way to the dull but morning-brightened interior of a mountain cabin.

Before him stood Canton Otie, hands still tied behind his back, ankles still bound together.

Lippy came to his feet and swung up the shotgun, aiming it at Canton's middle. "Don't you try nothing, Canton! Don't you try nothing!" Then he lowered the shotgun, suddenly feeling ridiculous. What in the world could a trussed-up fool try, anyway?

"My ankles hurt, Lippy. The ropes are too tight."

"I told you already, I can't loosen them. Devil Jack will have my hide if I do."

"Why are you doing this to me, Lippy? I don't understand."

"It's the money, Canton. That's all. Nothing against you. Nobody wants you to get hurt. Devil Jack just wants his money back, that's all."

"Dex's money is Devil Jack's money?"

"That's right. He took it off of Wade Murchison in that railroad car. Devil Jack's told me all about it."

"But why are you helping Devil Jack?"

"Because if I help him, he's going to share some of that money with me."

"But why are you doing this to me? Why are you making me stay tied up?"

"We had to, Canton. You see, Dex was getting ready to leave town. He'd take that money away, go off somewhere, and Jack would never get it back."

"Is Devil Jack a friend of yours?"

"Yes. I reckon he is."

"But you're my cousin, Lippy. You're kinfolk to me, and to Dex, too. Don't kinfolk count more than just being friends? Dex always said it did."

"Why don't you just sit down and shut up, Canton? I can't answer all your questions."

"Is Devil Jack going to hurt me?"

Lippy didn't know the answer, but he said, "No. I don't know why he would. It's Dex he wants."

"I thought you said all he wants is Dex's money."

"I'm tired of talking. Go back to your chair and sit down like you ought to. If Devil Jack comes in and finds you out of your chair, he'll not be happy about it."

"You won't let him hurt Dex, will you?"

"Sit down! Now! And shut up."

"Where's Devil Jack?"

"I don't know. Maybe out watching, waiting for Dex to come."

"Dex will come, won't he?"

"He'll come. Because of you. That's why we had to do it, Canton. You're the only one he'd have come for. Now, go sit down."

Canton slept that night, but poorly. His bonds hurt him, wrist and ankle, and the dream of the pursuing shadow was more vivid than ever before. He awakened from it and found himself staring into the grim face of Devil Jack Murchison. It was morning.

"You ain't changed much, Canton," Devil Jack said. "I remember when your brother was trying to join me and Wade's gang. You looked just the same then."

"I got to pee."

"Lippy'll take you outside."

"Are you going to hurt me, Devil Jack?"

"Why would you ask that? You aim to give me reason to hurt you?"

"I don't understand all this. I don't know why you're being mean to me."

"It's simple. Dex has my money. He has no right to it. I've kidnapped you, and I'm holding you here, and later this morning Dex will come in, bringing all that money with him, and he'll give me the money, in exchange for you."

"And what will you do then?"

Devil Jack stood, turning to Lippy, who was eating stale bread at a broken-down table in the far corner. "Lippy. Take the half-wit outside for a piss. Not far. Keep him close to the cabin." He turned again to Canton. "Your brother's a murderer. Did you know that?"

"He ain't!"

"He killed my brother. Wade. You remember Wade, don't you?"

"He *didn't*! Dex didn't kill nobody!"

"He shot Wade in that train. And when Wade didn't die, he went to Bluefield and smothered him under a pillow. Murdered him. And that same night, there was another man killed in Bluefield. Stabbed in the throat in an alley. Hell, maybe Dex killed him, too."

"Dex ain't that way. Dex don't kill nobody!"

"Believe what you want. But I know the truth, and I intend that your brother's going to pay the price for it. He owes me. And not just that money he stole."

"You're going to kill him?"

"What do you think?"

"Don't kill him! Please don't kill him!"

Devil Jack turned away, went to the window, and stared out.

Lippy came to Canton's bedside. "Come on, Canton. Let's step outside."

Canton rolled over, his back toward Lippy. His shoulders began to shake.

"Suit yourself, then. Pee the bed, if that suits you."
He went back and sat down again.

Devil Jack looked at Lippy. "Will he come?"

"Dex? He'll come."

Devil Jack looked back out the window. "You'd better hope he does. Because I've trusted you when you say this will fetch him. And if it don't happen that way, I'm holding this to your account."

Lippy stared at the stale bread but didn't touch it. For some reason he suddenly wasn't hungry anymore.

Chapter Sixteen

Lippy left the house half an hour later and wandered into a thicket to, as he had put it, "take care of a bit of business." When he rose, hitching his trousers, he looked about, frowning and sensing something, and hurried back to the cabin.

"Something's happening," he said. "I think maybe he's out there."

Devil Jack had been dozing in the corner, hat pulled over his face. Now he sat up and tossed the hat into the corner. "You saw him?"

"Heard him. Heard something, at least."

"Lippy!"

The call made Lippy start with surprise. The voice was Dex Otie's. Canton, hearing it, sat up on the bed with the eagerness of a pup before feeding.

"Lippy! You in there? Holler back!"

Lippy looked at Devil Jack for direction.

"Go ahead. Lift the window and yell out. But don't show yourself."

Following Jack's instructions, Lippy positioned himself to one side of the window and turned his mouth toward it. "I'm here, Dex!"

"What about Canton?"

"He's here, too."

"If he's hurt, Lippy, I swear I'll—"

"He ain't hurt. He's fine."

A pause. "Where's Devil Jack?"

Lippy looked at his companion again, uncertain. Devil Jack said, "Ask him why he wants to know."

"Why you want to know, Dex?"

"Because I don't trust you. For all I know, you dug out of Canton all about our trouble with Devil Jack and such, and decided to play you a little trick. Haul Canton off and kill him, leave a letter like Devil Jack had come along and kidnapped him, and wait for me to bring you the money, with Devil Jack nowhere near!"

"I don't trust him," Devil Jack said, nearly in a whisper. "Let him talk a bit more before we reveal anything."

"Dex, you can trust me! I ain't pulling no tricks!"

"I don't even know that Canton's there. Let me see him. At the door. And let me talk to him."

Devil Jack nodded his permission, then stepped back farther into the interior shadows. Lippy freed Canton's ankles from their bonds and hustled him off the bed and up to the door, handling him roughly now. "No funny stuff, no tricks," he said. "You tell him we been treating you good."

Canton blinked into the brilliant sky as the door swung open. Stiff and sore from his confinement, he had difficulty standing straight. He looked about for Dex and didn't see him. Dex's voice boomed out from some-

where in the rocky little aspen grove ahead of the cabin.
"Canton! You all right, boy?"

"I'm all right, Dex. My feet's asleep and tingly. They
had me tied up on—" He cut off as Lippy nudged him
sharply from the side.

"Is Devil Jack in there, Canton?"

"Go ahead and tell him," Devil Jack said.

"Yes, Dex. He's here."

And just as he said that, Canton caught sight of movement off in the trees toward his right, as if someone was
circling down toward the cabin. But when Dex replied,
his voice came from the same spot as before, almost
directly ahead.

Dex had brought someone else with him, and whoever
it was was making his way on the sneak toward the
cabin. A similar motion to the left caught Canton's eye,
but he held himself back from reacting. He shifted his
eyes that way and for half a second clearly saw an armed
man dart across a gap between two hiding rocks.

"Tell Devil Jack that if he wants his money, he's
going to have to let you go free first."

Suddenly Canton was jerked back into the cabin interior. Devil Jack Murchison took his place, though only
briefly, and kept his body mostly shielded behind the
frame of the door. His gravelly voice boomed. "That
ain't the deal, Dex! You ain't in no position to change
terms, not if you want this half-wit to stay alive!"

"Don't you threaten me, Jack! You ain't going to kill
Canton. You ain't even going to hurt him. 'Cause if you
do, there'll be not a cent of that money reach your hand
ever again!"

"This ain't just about the money! This is about Wade!
You murdered him, you sorry bastard!"

"This ain't about Wade, and you know it! A man like
you, it's about the money. It's always about the
money!"

153

"Don't count on that!" Devil Jack replied. He reached back and yanked Canton up and into the door again, and pressed the muzzle of a .44 Colt revolver under his chin. "You play games with me, Dex, and right before your eyes I'll blow your brother's brains to the sky, what he's got of them!"

Canton wet his pants and began making gurgling sounds in his throat.

"You so much as hurt him, Devil Jack, and I'll see you dead! You hear me? I'll see you dead!"

There was motion to the left, just within Devil Jack's field of view. He jerked, stared, and saw a swarthy figure drop into hiding behind a log, then rise slowly to peer above it.

"Damn you!" Jack bellowed at the unseen Dex Otie. "You damned, cheating, betraying..." He fired off a shot at the figure behind the log, sending chips flying, and tugged at Canton, trying to bring him back inside.

In his hiding place among the aspens, Dex swore. His hired gunmen had sworn they wouldn't make their presence known until the most opportune moment.

At the cabin, meanwhile, Canton Otie had not been pulled inside. Devil Jack's hand had slipped, and for a second or two Canton stood transfixed but unencumbered, bound only at the wrists, but his feet free.

When he realized this, and when the gunman behind the log, engraged by Devil Jack's shot, rose, fired down at the cabin, and almost struck him instead of Devil Jack, Canton bolted forward, running for the aspen grove and his hidden brother...

... who remained hidden no more. Seeing Canton coming toward him, he rose from his refuge. "Run hard, Canton! Run hard!"

Canton couldn't run hard. His feet still tingled from hours of constricted circulation; his muscles were soft from forced confinement to the bed. He moved terribly slowly. . . .

Devil Jack Murchison came to the door, raised a rifle, and aimed it at Canton. He'd lost a brother because of Dex Otie; he'd not see Dex now enjoy the victory of regaining his own brother. Jack's finger squeezed, slowly, his sights lined up squarely on the area just between Canton's shoulder blades.

A shot from behind the log to his left missed Devil Jack but caught just a bit of the grip of the rifle, throwing off his aim just as he squeezed the trigger. The slug whizzed high, zipping past Canton's ear but not striking him.

The gunman behind the log fired again, and Devil Jack felt a sting in his thigh. Roaring, he wheeled about as blood gushed down his leg. The gunman was about to squeeze off his third shot when Devil Jack beat him to it. The top of the gunman's head came off, accompanied by a fine, red spray.

Canton, meanwhile, kept running. He was almost to Dex now. Dex reached out to him, urging him to safety.

The second hidden gunman, until this moment unknown to Devil Jack, let out a yell as he saw his partner take the bullet through the head. He rose and fired down at the house, a rain of bullets smacking the wood around Devil Jack, sending him ducking back inside, where he tripped over Lippy, who was cowering on his elbows and knees, forearms wrapped over his head, face in the floor, rump in the air.

Devil Jack came to his feet, kicked Lippy soundly, cursed him even more so. "You going to fight, you sorry coward, or you going to lie there getting in my way?"

"I can't fight!" Lippy declared. "I never been a fighting man. . . . I ain't got it in me."

"Then you ain't no use to me," Devil Jack replied. "Get the hell out of here."

"I can't go out there! They're shooting at us!"

"You go, or I'll shoot you dead right here!"

Whining and moaning, Lippy got up and crept toward the door. With Devil Jack out of sight, there was a momentary lull in the shooting. Lippy gave a glance back at Devil Jack, gulped hard, and came out the door. "Don't shoot!" he yelled, hands stuck straight up in the air. "Don't shoot me, nobody! I'm just—"

The lone remaining hired gunman squeezed a trigger, and Lippy Blake did a spectacular turning fall to his left, arms swirling straight out and around like those of a dancer performing a graceful spin. He collapsed twitching to the ground and did not move again.

"Lippy's dead!" Canton said, having seen it all. Dex had not, being occupied in trying to free Canton's hands from their bonds. "Lippy's dead! Lippy's dead! Lippy's—"

"Hush, Canton, hush! Don't get worked up on me now." Dex glanced below, saw Lippy's unmoving body. "I be damned! So he is."

"I'm scared, Dex. I'm so scared—"

"Nothing to be scared of now. You got away from them. What a run, boy! I'm proud of you."

The shooting renewed below. Dex studied the situation. "I don't believe this is a hire job now, Canton. My gunman down there is mad. Hear him cussing and talking, going on so mad? It's personal now. Devil Jack killed his partner."

"Who is that man?"

"Just a fellow I hired to help me get Devil Jack. Him and his partner. And you know, boy, I believe he *will* get him! Is there a back way out of that cabin?"

"No. Just the one door."

"Windows on the back and sides?"

"No. Just the front. I'm scared, Dex. I want to go."

"We are going. You and me both, and now. And

we're getting out of Denver. Lippy's dead, and Devil Jack will be soon enough. He's cornered. But when it's pay time for my hired gun yonder, he's going to have a bit of trouble finding us. We'll be already on our way.''

''Where?''

''To wherever it is we'll go, and God only knows where that'll be. It don't really matter. What does matter is that we still got most our money, Devil Jack will be dead, and now there'll be nobody chasing us, nobody at all left behind to know where we'll be. We're free and clear, Canton, *if* we can get away from here really fast.''

''We'll ride like the devil, Dex. Like you said that time. Ride like the devil.''

''That's right. You up to it?''

''Yes.''

''Then come on.''

''Dex . . .''

''What?''

''Did you really do what they said, and kill Devil Jack's brother?''

''No, Canton. I didn't. You think I'd do such a thing? It's just a wild story Devil Jack is telling to make me look bad.'' Dex glanced below at the continuing gun battle. ''He won't be around to tell it much longer, though. Good thing, huh?''

''Let's go, Dex.''

''Good idea, boy. Let's do.''

They rose and headed back through the aspens to the place where horses waited. After mounting, and stringing the horses of the two hired gunmen along behind, they rode away and out, putting miles behind them as fast as they could.

A week and many miles later, Dex chanced upon a copy of a Denver newspaper in a saloon. It carried an account of the aftermath of an apparent gun battle at an old and normally abandoned cabin in a secluded valley outside Denver. Three bodies were found there, it said, all dead from gunshot wounds. One was Horace "Lippy" Blake, a small-time criminal and Denver gambler. The other two were not known by name, but were identified by authorities as two well-known gunmen-for-hire, wanted in at least six states, and believed to be the assassins of . . . and the article went on to string out several names, none of whom Dex had ever heard of.

He scoured the story for any mention of the finding of a fourth body, but there was none. He couldn't believe it. Devil Jack had survived.

At first this generated panic, but he calmed himself by recalling several important facts. First, he and Canton had made a clean break, left no trail, and most important, had revealed no plans to anyone about where they would be going. This time there was no Mary Alice McGee to be found and forced to reveal any damning facts. Second, the nation was vast; he and Canton could easily vanish into it, so deeply Devil Jack would never be able to find them if he spent the rest of his days trying.

Third, Devil Jack certainly *wouldn't* spend his days chasing them. He'd give up the pursuit, believing that even if he did find Dex Otie by some miracle, the effort would surely outlast the money. And whatever sentiment Devil Jack might attach to his efforts, Dex was sure that at heart the motivator was the money, far more so than any drive to avenge his brother's murder.

Fourth, he and Canton wouldn't be around to be found. They'd change their names—their last names, at least. They'd take up shaving regularly, dressing better, different. Dex would change the part of his hair, maybe buy some dye and give it a new color. They'd leave behind the criminal life they'd known, settle into a good town somewhere, go into legitimate business, and make the money they had left blossom and grow into a continuing wealth that would be with them the rest of their days. Let Devil Jack search for them among the dives and the saloons, if he wanted! They'd not be there to find—not, at least, as customers. Dex just might open himself a saloon somewhere, make money from his salooning, instead of pouring it down a hole.

Life was going to change for the Otie brothers. Going to improve. No more drifting, living in the saddle, making whatever sorry living could be found in petty thefts and petty gambling. No more of that. Life wasn't only going to change. It was going to get better . . . and this time without Devil Jack Murchison trailing after them like that black shadow in Canton's dream.

Dex left that newspaper where he found it, and never told Canton what it said. He'd let Canton believe that Devil Jack was dead. No harm in it.

They moved on, letting the roads and trails take them where they led. And where they led, it turned out, was Kansas.

Part IV
Chase

Chapter Seventeen

November 1885; Dodge City, Kansas

He ran down the middle of the street, laughing, children at his heels, their young voices chanting after him in rough chorus: " 'Cant' write, 'Cant' read, 'Cant' do a thing . . . 'Cant' write, 'Cant' read, 'Cant' do a thing . . . 'Cant' go to school, 'cause Cant's a fool . . .''

On the boardwalks, men and women frowned at the odd parade, disliking the cruelty of the children to a poor, mentally slow man, but not disliking it enough to say anything about it. The man known in Dodge City as Cant Wilson swept past them, that endless, foolish grin on his face, as if he didn't comprehend that he was being mocked.

They turned onto Front Street and past the Junction saloon, and on down to the narrow-fronted Wilson House, upon which hung a sign declaring WILSON HOUSE DRUGS—ICED LAGER BEER AVAILABLE FOR MEDICINAL

USE. A smaller sign below it read "Dexter Wilson, Resident Proprietor." And just below that, scrawled onto the wall, some young wag had freshly scribbled in the words "Cant Wilson, Resident Half-wit."

Cant bounded off the street and onto the boardwalk, rushing toward the saloon door, almost bowling over a man who was exiting. "Watch out, there!" the man bellowed at him, his breath a beery gust. Just another man with medical needs, taking his "medicine" at what was in fact a saloon, but which presented itself as a drugstore in order to remain within the boundaries of Kansas's five-year-old temperance law. All down the streets of Dodge were other similar institutions, all of them selling spirits and functioning just like saloons, but under the guise of restaurants, apothecaries, billiard halls, even art galleries.

Dex Otie, now known to all as Dex Wilson, appeared in the doorway. "Mr. Bailey, sir, I'm very sorry. I apologize for my brother."

The children who had been chasing Canton scattered and vanished. They'd faced Dex Wilson's wrath before.

"Well, no harm done," Bailey said. "But you need to tell him"—he probed a finger at Canton—"to watch where he's going."

"I'll speak with him right away, sir," Dex replied, talking, like Bailey, as if Canton weren't already there to hear it all. "And next time you come in, the first beer is on the house."

"Well! All right, then." Bailey shook Dex's hand. "You're a good businessman, Mr. Wilson."

"Good day to you, sir."

When Wilson was gone, Dex thumbed toward the new "sign" on the wall, with the slighting reference to Canton. "See that? It calls you a half-wit, boy. Makes fun of you. Just like them children was doing. They're mocking you, and yet you run on ahead of them with that big stupid grin on your face, like it's all a game!''

Canton flinched back. Tirades from Dex, such as this one, were becoming very common lately, had been coming with greater frequency ever since he and Dex had settled in Dodge three years back, when Dex had expended what remained of the Murchison money to get the Wilson House started.

"I'm sorry. They didn't mean no harm, them children."

"No harm? They're making fun of you, boy! Can't you see that? Probably it's one of them who painted this up on the wall here! You're a joke to them, Canton. Just a joke!''

Canton looked sheepishly around, embarrassed to be receiving a scolding on a public street boardwalk, where everyone could see and hear. "I'm sorry, Dex."

"Get on in here. Floor needs sweeping. Maybe you can do that without making a bigger fool of yourself than you are. Think so?''

"Yes."

"Then do it. We're letting all the cold air in standing here in the door. And for God's sake, don't play along when them children taunt you. Have some respect for yourself! I tell you, Canton, sometimes I don't know why I put up with keeping you around. You embarrass me. It was one thing back when we was riding about the country, free and clear, but another thing altogether now that I'm in business. You make me look bad, and I expect you to do better. You understand me?''

"Yes."

"Good. Now, get to sweeping. And don't miss the corners this time.''

Dex and Canton resided in a little cluster of four rooms above a drugstore—an authentic one—across the street from Dex's make-believe one. In these small chambers the pair lived out their increasingly divergent lives. Dex was a different man from the brother Canton had known all his life. Better in a way—now a businessman rather than a drifting criminal—but other than that, worse. Or so Canton saw it. Dex drank now, almost all the time he wasn't working, and sometimes when he was. He was gruff, unsmiling, preoccupied.

Worst of all, Canton was beginning to believe his brother no longer liked him. After today, he was more sure of it than ever.

He sat by the window, staring out onto Front Street, watching the people pass up and down the walks. Many saloons and dance halls in Dodge stayed open all around the clock, and in fact Dex's place had done the same for the first couple of years, but eventually Dex had been forced to let go the extra help required to operate the business twenty-four hours a day. Not making enough money, he'd explained to Canton. Now the saloon closed at midnight, usually. Sometimes sooner, such as tonight. Dex, in some mysterious fit of dissatisfaction with everything, had abruptly closed the place down about five in the evening, earlier than ever before, and dragged Canton home.

Now Dex was drinking back in his room, and Canton was staring at the street and brooding.

He decided that maybe he liked it better the way it was before, when he and Dex had used their real last name and had been free drifters. It had been difficult to find enough to eat, and it had been hard to sleep on the ground as much as they had to in those days, but still it had been better.

Up until Devil Jack had started chasing them, that is. Canton still vividly recalled the terror of his captivity and the closeness of his escape. He dreamed about it a lot . . . and lately, he had been dreaming about that pursuing shadow again, the one that ate Dex alive. The shadow that even the dull-witted Canton had come to realize was a mental picture of Devil Jack Murchison.

But Devil Jack was dead, as far as Canton knew, killed by that hired gunman of Dex's. So the dream was nothing but foolishness, nothing to worry about.

Yet he did worry.

Canton had been staring at the ground for the last several minutes. His gaze drifted upward now, toward the sky . . . but paused when he saw something odd at the Junction saloon.

Smoke. Curling out around the edges of a closed upper window. Canton peered closely, then rose.

"Dex! Dex! There's fire!"

Dex's drunken mumble wafted from his bedroom. Cant ran back there and found him lying on the bed, an empty whiskey flask at his side. "Dex, there's fire! Over at the Junction!"

Dex grunted but didn't really seem to hear. From the street outside Canton heard the noise of men running and shouting, and the clang of a fire bell.

"Wake up, Dex! You got to wake up!"

But Dex wouldn't. Canton hovered in panicked indecision, then gave up and left Dex's room, closing the door behind him. He grabbed his coat off its peg beside the main door and, throwing it on hurriedly, scurried out, down, and into the rising tumult outside.

He could smell the smoke clearly before reaching the street. The fire was spreading fast—and Dex's saloon was right in its path.

The next morning, a hungover Dex stood on the street before what had been his place of business, and wept. Canton, having never seen his brother cry, even as a boy, didn't know what to make of it. He cowered back as if Dex were a stranger.

167

"It's gone, Canton," Dex said at length. "All gone. Everything."

And so it was. All that remained of the Wilson House was a single fragment of the front wall—the part, ironically, that held the sign listing Dex Wilson as proprietor, and the false sign with the insult about Canton.

Dex was not alone in his loss. Dodge City had lost about a block of its most established businesses, from a jewelry store to the Delmonico restaurant, from furniture stores to scads of saloons, from an opera house to a theater. Even the famed Wright & Co. building, where many a weary cowboy had outfitted himself in new clothing at the end of long trail drives was destroyed.

"You can build it back, Dex," Canton said. "Just get some wood and nails and a hammer, and—"

"We can't build it back," Dex snapped. "No insurance."

"What's that?"

"It's something that you got to have to rebuild if a building gets burned down. And I ain't got it."

Canton stared at his own name scrawled on that fragment of wall. "What'll we do now, Dex?"

"I don't know." He waved toward the burned-out block. "Why the hell didn't you rouse me when this fire started?"

"I tried to. I really did."

Dex turned away and headed back across the street. "You should have tried harder," he said.

That night, Canton heard Dex say things that pleased him and gave him hope—things that almost made him glad, secretly, that the fire had come.

Dex's voice was gentle again, like the old days. It was that way all too rarely anymore. "You remember Montgomery Harper, Canton?"

"No."

"Well, he's a Texan, a very rich man whose daughter I saved from some mistreatment by a couple of drunks out behind the saloon, when her father was in town on business and she'd come along for the ride."

"I remember now."

"He was mighty grateful to me for that . . . though the truth is, Canton, that them men were too drunk to do what they was threatening to that girl. And to tell you the truth, I think she'd flirted with them so much they thought she *wanted* them to be that way with her. But anyway, old man Harper said he was mighty beholden to me for saving her, and that if ever I was in need of anything down Texas way, to look him up." He paused. "I believe I'm going to do that."

"We're going to Texas?"

"May as well. Nothing to stay here for, and all the money's gone. Every cent we got off that train, Canton, it's gone. I invested it to get the saloon started, but the saloon never gave enough back except to break us even, and that just some of the time. Hell, I'm halfway glad to be shut of the place. Maybe times will be brighter in Texas."

"What kind of work would you do?"

"I don't know. Harper's mostly in cattle and such."

"You'd be a cattleman?"

"Not likely. Don't know nothing much about it. But Harper owns a passel of stores and saloons, and he's got to have folks to run them. I do know about that. That's one thing Dodge give me, experience in running a business."

"I'll get work in Texas, too. Maybe *I'll* become a cattleman."

"Boy, you ain't going to be nothing but Canton Wilson. You'll stick with me, do what I tell you, and stay out of folks' way once we hit Texas."

Canton looked disappointed. He asked, "Dex, why

we still have to use a made-up last name? Devil Jack ain't around no more to hurt us. Why can't I be Canton Otie again?''

Dex studied his brother thoughtfully, sucked in a deep breath, and said, ''There's something I ain't told you. Didn't see the need to scare you. But Devil Jack didn't get killed in that gun battle back at Denver.''

''He's *alive*?''

''Unless he's been killed or died since then, I reckon he is. That's why we used the false names here, and why we'll use them once we hit Texas. Just in case, you know. Hell, we'd have used false first names, too, except I knew you'd never be able to keep them straight. You'd call the wrong name sometime or other and knock the lid off the whole secret.''

''Devil Jack is alive.'' Canton said it flatly, staring at the floor, thinking about his recent dreams of the pursuing shadow. He looked up sharply. ''Dex, is he out there? On the street?''

''Of course he ain't. We been in Dodge three years now, and we ain't seen the first sign of him. Hell, he's probably off in California or Maine or Oregon or God only knows where! I doubt he'd bother to come for us even if he knew where we was to be found.''

''Why not?''

''Because by now he'd figure the money was surely gone—which indeed it is. Three years is a long time. I'd say he's clean forgot about us.''

''Then why can't we use our real names again?''

Dex paused, then said, ''Just in case he ain't forgot us after all.''

They possessed little beyond their clothing, some personal items, and a bit of furniture. Dex sold what he could and with the money bought himself and Canton a railroad ticket. They left Dodge behind, the last image of it to linger in Dex's mind being that pitiful-looking remnant of a burned wall, with his name and Canton's.

He'd had some big dreams for Kansas. They had come to almost nothing.

In Texas, though, things would be different. Harper had meant it when he invited Dex to call on him if he needed anything. Dex could tell.

He only hoped Harper wasn't one of those forgetful sorts. If this prospect didn't turn out, all he and Canton could do was go back to the drifting life they had shared for so many years. He didn't want to do that at all. He'd grown awfully fond of sleeping in a real bed and eating his breakfast on a table.

The train chugged on, heading out the Atchison, Topeka, and Santa Fe line, carrying them away. Canton stared through the dirty window back toward the receding town. Dex didn't look back at all.

A few years earlier, the people of Dodge would have identified the newcomer as a buffalo hunter. He had the look about him, the broad shoulders, big body, hulking way of sitting his saddle.

He rode onto Front Street, studying the charred remnants of the buildings that had been gutted by the fire. He hadn't heard about the fire: He seldom read papers, even when he had the chance. He wondered what had sparked it, and how much had been lost. Not that it mattered. Wasn't really his concern.

On down the street, he pulled his weary, decrepit horse to a halt and squinted at the remains of one wall. In a whisper he formed the names he read on a sign there: Dex Wilson . . . Cant Wilson . . . but as he read them, only half his mouth moved. The left half was frozen, unmoving, like the drooping eye above it.

A boy ran nearby, one of the same ones who had pursued Canton down the street only a few days before.

171

"Boy!" the man called. "Come here for a minute."

The boy complied, but suspiciously, because this man looked strange and dangerous. "What you need, mister?"

"Them names on that wall. Dex Wilson and Cant Wilson. You know who they are?"

"Yes, sir. Mr. Dex Wilson was the man who run this saloon until it burned down the other night. The other, Cant, that's his brother."

"A half-wit, that says. Is that true?"

"Yes, sir."

"Two brothers, one named Dex, the other Cant, and Cant being a half-wit. Tell me this, boy: Is 'Cant' short for something?"

"Well, sir, I believe it's short for Canton."

The big man nodded; the stiffened lip quivered, the nostrils flared, the fire in the one good eye flared.

"Tell me, son, where I can find this here Dex Wilson?"

"You know him, mister?"

"I do believe so. From about three years back."

"Well, I'm sorry to tell you, but he's gone. He and his brother left town after the fire. Hopped on a train bound for Texas."

The big man drew in a deep breath. "Damn!" he said. "Gone to Texas. . . . Do you know where, boy?"

"As I hear it, sir, somewhere in east Texas. That's all I know. He was talking to some of the men in town about how he was going to look up some rich man who owed him a favor, and get work from him."

"East Texas," the big man repeated.

The boy lingered, looking expectant. The big man turned his harsh eye upon him. "Get off with you, boy. If you're waiting for money, I got none to give. I'm a poor man."

The boy turned and ran off. Devil Jack Murchison

watched him go, then turned his eye toward the burned-out wall again. "It's been a long time, Dex," he said. "I figured I'd never chance upon you again. But I got lucky, huh? About time. About time."

Devil Jack spent two days in Dodge City, selling a pistol and his old horse. Then he bought himself a train ticket and headed for Texas.

Chapter Eighteen

Seven months later; Harperville, Texas

Dex leaned back on the big chair on the vast and sprawling porch that surrounded the big house of Montgomery Harper, and sipped a delicious whiskey. He couldn't suppress a smile. Life was good. Better than good. Sometimes it was downright miraculous.

Just over half a year back, he'd left Dodge City as a destitute and bitter man, hoping against hope that Montgomery Harper would not only remember him but give him some kind of job in one of his many enterprises. Things had fallen together beyond Dex's wildest hopes. Dex came to Harper at just the right time. The man who managed one of Harper's biggest businesses, a general store with a big saloon attached right in the heart of the East Texas town of Harperville, had died of something or another, and Harper was hard-pressed to find an adequate replacement. And just then, as luck would have it, was when Dex had come knocking on Harper's office door, reminding him of an old favor done his daughter, and a promise made in the wake of it.

Harper was as good as his word, and Dex walked right into a fine job, managing not one but two businesses, and finding out on top of it all that Harper didn't keep any too close an eye on his own books. Dex had started skimming cash for himself a month into his duties, and had continued ever since.

And that wasn't even the best of it.

The best of it was Jeannie.

Jeannie Harper. The same young woman Dex had rescued from would-be rapists behind his own saloon in Dodge was now Jeannie Harper Wilson, his wife.

They married because they had to. Montgomery Harper insisted on it. When he discovered his daughter, unwed, was well along the way to delivering offspring, he'd forced a wedding. Never mind that Dex might not have been the father—the way Jeannie lived her life, there were any number of candidates—Montgomery Harper's desire was that his daughter have a husband, so that his first grandchild would not come into the world a bastard.

It was ironic, though, how that turned out. Only two weeks past the wedding, Jeannie miscarried. Perhaps by accident, perhaps not. Dex didn't know. But suddenly here he was, married to the beautiful wild-as-a-cat daughter of the most wealthy tycoon in all Texas, living in a fine suite of rooms in the big house, operating two successful businesses that gave him good pay and even better embezzled dollars.

Dex grinned, thinking about it, and lifted his glass in toast to that wonderfully providential fire back in Dodge. Without that fire, he'd never have come to Texas.

Even Canton had it good here. Within Dex's view from where he sat was a small but snug house on the corner of the mansion property. Canton's home, given to him by the largesse of Dex's new father-in-law. Montgomery Harper seemed to like Canton, or at least find him interesting, kind of an intriguing human mascot to have about the place. He gave Canton not only a home but also work in the big kitchen of the house. Canton was turning into quite a fine cook and plate dresser, under the tutelage of the elderly black cook, his wife, and three Mexican helpers.

Dex was glad that old man Harper was willing to accommodate Canton. It was quite a relief, really, not having to share quarters with him anymore. He'd watched over Canton all his life, devoted himself to him, been more than patient with his annoying half-wit ways. He was more than happy to be freed of at least part of the burden of seeing to his welfare. A man had only one life, after all, and it was nothing but cussed foolishness to expend it all on someone else's behalf.

That latter bit of philosophy was something being reinforced in Dex every day by none other than his own dear wife. He'd never known a more thoroughly self-centered human being than Jeannie—yet she had a way of making self-centeredness seem the most sensible and appealing philosophy in the world. She'd put Dex to thinking on levels he'd never thought on before. If this world was all there is, and this life the only one a person was given, why shouldn't it be devoted at every level to one's own personal welfare? Why, for example, should Dex have spent all the years he had caring for Canton? Why should he have sacrificed so much just for his brother's welfare?

Well, Dex had answered her, just because he *is* my brother. Family. And family ought to take care of one another . . . ought'n they?

Why? Jeannie had asked. Why should I give up a bit of what's good for me for the sake of somebody else, just because that somebody else shares my bloodline?

Dex had argued with her to begin with. Though he wasn't a moral man by any stretch, he found her cold and calculating attitude appalling. But as time went by, she was wearing him down. Making him wonder if maybe she wasn't correct after all.

He remembered a thing he'd said to Canton more than once over the years: "Right" is for old women and preachers. Maybe that statement was even more true than he had thought.

He sipped his drink until it was empty, then rose and went back into the house.

Jeannie lay close beside him, her body warm and soft against his, the afterglow of expended passion still lingering around and upon them.

She stroked his face with an extended finger, playful.

"Father's feeling a little sick today. Did you know that?"

"Heard one of the servants mention it this morning."

"Just a little sick . . . but he'll get better. He always does. Father's a strong and healthy man." She paused. "Too bad."

He twisted his head slightly and looked at her. "What? You *want* your father to be sickly?"

"Why shouldn't I? Sickly men die sooner."

"Lord a'mighty, woman! Don't you even love your own father?"

"I love his money more."

He pondered her, amazed anew by this woman he'd taken as wife. "Are you thinking about your inheritance? Is that it?"

"What else would it be? When Father passes on, I'm going to be a wealthy woman. And you, being my husband, will be a wealthy man. Don't tell me you haven't thought about that!"

Of course he'd thought about it. It was the very reason he'd been willing to comply when Montgomery Harper insisted he marry her. "I guess it's crossed my mind a time or two. But I never thought about wishing ill health on the old man because of it."

"Just think what it would be like if all Father's money and lands and businesses and herds—if it all was ours! Can you imagine the life we'd live?"

"Seems to me we're living a pretty good life as it is. Hell, Jeannie, a year ago I was just squeaking by in Kansas, running a saloon that did well to break even every month! Now I've got good work, good money, and you for my wife. And when the old man does pass on, whenever that is, there'll be even more for me. I'm satisfied."

"That's your problem, Dex. You're satisfied way too easy. You don't know how to dream big . . . or how to make those dreams come true."

"What are you talking about?"

"I'm talking about, what if there was a way to make that inheritance pass to us sooner than it would if we let things happen on their own? I don't want to be an old woman before that inheritance comes to me."

"Jeannie, if I didn't know better, I'd think you were talking about killing your father."

"Maybe not *me* doing it . . . maybe somebody else." She snuggled a bit closer to him.

"Wait a minute. . . . If you're suggesting that I'm going to murder your father for you, then you can just—"

"Oh, no, Dex, not *you*! That wouldn't be very clever, would it! The way to do it would be for someone else to do the job . . . or to make it look like an accident that wasn't anybody's fault, or—"

"Hold up, lady. Hold up right there. I don't like this kind of talk. This is dangerous, this kind of thinking.

You're sounding like this might be something you'd really do!''

"Maybe it would be."

"I don't want to hear nothing more about it."

She looked at him intently, her face inches from his. "Dex, think about it. If we could get rid of Father, and do it cleverly, so that no one could tell what happened, and if we could do it so that maybe your idiot brother took the blame, we'd be free and clear and *rich*—''

"Damnation! You mean you'd want to use Canton for your scapegoat? I'll not hear of such! I'll not even think of it!''

"*Do* think of it, Dex! Do! There are ways it could be done, easy ways. I know of a poison that you can use that they say can't be found out at all, one that makes a person die in a natural kind of way that no one suspects. A very pretty little poison. And I know how to get it.''

"No. No."

"Put it into food, they say you can't even taste it.''

"No!''

"And Canton works in the kitchen, dresses the plates . . .''

"I said *no*! I mean it, woman. I'd never do such a thing! Canton is my brother!''

"Think about it, Dex. What it would be like to be rich and free . . . and rid of Canton.''

"No!''

"You and me, rich, free—''

"No, I say!''

"Think about it.''

"I won't!''

But long past midnight, as Jeannie slept beside him, he did think about it. God help him, he thought about it a lot.

Two days later, Canton became sick. Dex went to his house to visit him and found him lying on his bed in vomit, too ill to get up and do anything about it.

Dex stood by the bedside, looking down at the pitiful man reclining in his own foulness, and a thought rose unbidden: *I hate him.*

Dex backed away, shocked by the thought. No, he didn't hate Canton. Canton was his brother, a man who, without him, would have no one and nothing. He'd spent his life devoted to Canton, sacrificing for him, always seeing to his welfare even when it was inconvenient. . . .

. . . And I'm sick of it. Tired of putting up with this hopeless idiot who'll be with me until I die, keeping me from ever getting anywhere, keeping me from ever really being free to enjoy myself without worrying about him. . . . I hate him. I truly do hate him.

He cleaned up Canton's mess, changed the linens, washed him off. Canton, feverish, babbled on about silly things, and about that familiar old pursuing shadow. Dex told him to shut up, but Canton was too sick to hear.

Dex left Canton's house and headed for the store in Harperville, thinking about the dark things Jeannie had talked about in the privacy of their bed. Thinking about them very hard.

Montgomery Harper came by the store that day. Not an uncommon occurrence, but today something was different. Harper always came first to Dex upon such occasions, cheerful and talking business and family. Today he didn't come to Dex at all, actually seemed to be trying to avoid encountering him. He slipped into the store, looked furtively about, and made for the office, entering and closing the door behind him. Dex watched it all, unseen, through a knothole in the wall between the main part of the store and the back stockroom.

He's come on the sneak! Dex thought. *The old coot*

don't want me to know he's here. Now, why would he do that?

The store was empty at the moment, so Dex crept across the floor toward the office. Peering through the little window in the door, he saw the gray-haired Harper digging into the big rolltop in the center of the office. He pulled out the big ledger that recorded all the financial goings-on of both the store and the saloon—a carefully doctored ledger that revealed little and hid much.

Dex watched with concern as Harper flipped through pages, reading closely, occasionally glancing about, and once looking right back at the door, causing Dex to have to jerk back to avoid being seen at the window.

Dex slipped back to the stockroom again, and there loosened his collar. A dampened collar, wet with the sweat of concern.

He knows. Somehow he knows I've been embezzling. Or at least he suspects.

Dex swore to himself and went back to the knothole. As he watched through it, Harper slipped out of the office, looked around, and headed out the front door.

Dex, so shaken he felt sick, plopped down on the floor and stared at the wall.

He knows. Somehow he knows . . . and as careful as I've been, he still might be able to dig out proof. I've got to do something. . . . I can't go to jail. I couldn't stand it.

That night he and Jeannie had a long talk in their bedroom. She knew about the embezzlement, had in fact been the one to suggest that Dex undertake it, and had directed him in how to go about it.

She seemed worried, too. If her father suspected something was asked with the books, he'd not rest until he had dug out the truth. He was that way, her father was.

"We've got to do something about this, Dex, before it all crumbles down on us."

"I know . . . but what?"

"I think you know what."

"Jeannie . . . I can't. I can't. It's too dangerous."

"If Father verifies that you've been embezzling from him, Dex, it will be pure hell for you. And for me. We *have* to do it now, Dex! Can't you see?"

He thought about it and nodded. "Yes. You're right. Now we have to do something. There's no choice anymore."

"You'll go along with me, then? Me and you together?"

A pause. "Yes."

"You'll leave it to me, how it's done?"

"Yes."

"And, Canton . . . can I use Canton, if I have to?"

The pause was much longer this time. Dex had the sense of standing at the edge of a dark new place that was somehow both repellent and attractive. He knew that if he stepped into that place, nothing would be as before. And he would never be able to take that step back.

"Well?" she urged. "Can I?"

He hung back a final moment, then took the step. "Yes," he said. "Yes, damn it, use Canton if you have to."

She smiled, and kissed him.

Chapter Nineteen

The kitchen was built in the old-fashioned style, out-doors, with a stone walkway leading from it to the house. Jeannie stood on the porch, watching the cooks and servants moving to and fro. Her hand was in the pocket of her dress apron, clutching a small vial of whitish-gray powder.

She waited, watched, her heart thumping. Dex was upstairs in their room, at the window, also watching. He was too nervous about all this even to come out, much less take part. This was fine with Jeannie, for it left the thrill of the actual *doing* of it to her alone.

Later tonight, her father would be dead, and the inheritance hers and Dex's—as long, at least, as she desired to keep Dex around. The same poison that worked to kill fathers could also kill husbands, and when the time came, she wouldn't hesitate to use it on Dex, if ever he grew wearisome.

She stepped off the porch when she saw the opportune

moment, and walked to the door of the stone kitchen.

Canton, recovered from his earlier illness, was inside, alone, putting the food onto the plates. Even Jeannie, who despised Canton because of his imbecility, had to admit he had an artistic touch when it came to dressing an attractive plate of food. Funny how sometimes even idiots could perform certain isolated tasks with remarkable skill.

"Canton."

He turned to her and gave a faltering smile. *He doesn't like me,* she thought. *How funny!*

"Can you step inside a moment? Dex wants to see you, up in our room."

"I'm supposed to be getting these plates ready for supper."

"You can do that when you come back. It'll only take a moment."

"Well, all right." He dusted his hands off on his apron and walked past her.

"Oh . . . Canton?"

"Yes?"

"Father mentioned something to me about how much he likes the way you decorate the plates with greenery every night. He said it adds a touch of elegance to the meals."

Canton smiled.

She glanced at the plates. "And he likes rose hip best of all. So tonight, you be sure there's rose hip on Father's plate—like that plate there. That plate, with the rose hip will be Father's. You understand that? The plate with the rose hip—no other."

"Yes."

"Oh . . . and don't put rose hip on any other plate but Father's. Put other things, flower petals and so on. He likes each plate to look different . . . and he likes his with rose hip."

Canton nodded. He'd had no notion until now that Mr. Harper even cared about the decorative touches of the plates. But if Harper did, Canton would do his best to comply. He liked pleasing his employer. He'd not only make sure his plate had rose hip to decorate it—he'd make sure Mr. Harper's plate was the prettiest, best-trimmed plate of the lot, right down to the way the food was laid out.

"Hurry on, Canton. Dex is waiting."

Canton left; Jeannie was alone. She moved swiftly to the plate with the rose hip, and into the heap of potatoes on it sprinkled a generous portion of the gray-white powder from the vial. With a spoon she stirred it in, then reshaped the potatoes as they had been before. Canton, as particular as he was with his plate decoration, would notice if things looked different.

She headed out the door just as some of the other servants came back in from the house. They gave her ready but cool greetings. She was not popular with them; she looked down on them, and they knew it.

Making sure no one was watching, she slipped over to Canton's little shed house, and in a drawer slipped the little vial, now containing only a trace of the powder she had mixed in her father's food.

She returned to the house and met Canton coming down the stairs.

"You saw Dex?"

"Yes . . . but he said never mind. He didn't have nothing to tell me after all."

"Oh? How odd." She started up the stairs past him.

"Miss Jeannie, is Dex sick?"

"I don't think so. Why?"

"He looked all pale just now. And he looked at me funny. Like something was wrong."

She smiled. "I can't imagine what would be wrong. I'm sure it's your imagination. Now you'd best get back to the kitchen. I'll go tell Dex it's almost time for supper.''

Dex indeed did look sickly. For a moment she despised him, standing there with that ghastly look on his face. Did the man have no backbone? Couldn't he see past the momentary tension of murder to the happy situation beyond? They were both on the verge of wealth—and Dex was about to drop the albatross of Canton from around his neck, besides. He should be happy, not edgy. Their scheme would not fail. It should be easy and foolproof to pin the death on a mental deficient such as Canton.

''Jeannie,'' he said as she entered, ''I don't know if I can go through with it. When Canton came up here, it was all I could do to look at him, knowing what we're doing to him.''

''Dex, who do you care for most? Canton, or me?''

''You, of course. You're my wife.''

''Then you'll do this for me. Think of what lies beyond, Dex! Money, power—and Father will be gone. He won't be digging through the the ledgers and books from his grave, will he! You'll have nothing to worry about for the rest of your days. And Canton will be off your hands forever! Just you and me . . . and all that money. That will be our life from now on. It's beautiful, isn't it!'' She came to him and put her arms around him.

''Yes. Yes. It will be. But Canton . . . I've never done a thing to hurt him before. God, Jeannie, what if they hang him?''

''What if they do? Will that take a cent out of your pocket?''

''You're a hard woman. Hard as iron.''

''It's the hard who survive. The hard who make it. And the weak who fail . . . or get hanged. Forget Canton, Dex. Think of yourself and me. Nothing else.''

He smiled at her, weakly, and nodded.

"Good. Now get ready. The meal is about to be served. The last supper, we should call it!" She laughed.

"So you did the job?"

"Oh, no. Not me. Remember, it isn't me who did it. It's Canton who poisoned the food. I mean . . . why else would the bottle of poison be hidden in Canton's little shed?"

"Yes. Right. Canton." He was trying his best to feel good about this.

"Come on, let's get to the table. I don't want to miss it when it happens."

She hurried out of the room. Dex followed. What a woman she was! As thoroughly wicked a person as he had ever known, but intriguing and enticing. She had a grip on him that he couldn't wrench free of if he tried.

It was going to be marvelous, he had to admit, living a life of wealth with his seductive, enticing, wicked wife. Nothing but luxury and pleasure for the rest of his days.

But Canton . . . poor Canton!

He forced that thought from his mind and made his way to the dining room, struggling not to let the turmoil inside him show.

Dex couldn't even taste the food. Every bite was forced, and he fancied that throughout the meal, old Harper was looking at him in a way he hadn't before.

Jeannie, for her part, was eating happily, her eye drifting every so often to that identifying decorative rose hip on her father's plate.

"Well, Dex," Montgomery Harper said after downing another huge bite of gravy-laden mashed potatoes, "I'm curious about how the store is faring these days. Profits still good?"

Why's he asking that? Dex wondered. *And when will that poison do its work?*

"Still good," he said. "Maybe a little better than last month."

"Uh-huh. I see. Everything all recorded, I'm sure, in the books?"

There was definitely something behind Harper's questions. "Yes, of course," Dex replied. He glanced at Jeannie, who gave him a quick smile as if to say, *Don't worry—it isn't going to matter in a little while, anyway.*

"How about the saloon?"

Dex fancied that there was an extra edge in that question. And it so happened that it was from the saloon that he had been doing most of his embezzlement. "Saloon's doing fine."

"That's good to hear. And all in the books, I reckon."

"Well, sure." He glanced again at Jeannie . . .

. . . who was looking back at him with the strangest of expressions. Her eyes widened, looked questioning, and then she stood, weakly and clumsily.

"Jeannie?" Dex came to his feet.

Harper stood and headed toward his daughter, extending his arm. She put her own arm toward him, but defensively, pushing away from him.

Dex reached her, put his arm around her shoulder. She shrugged him away, staggered away from the table. Her mouth was beginning to foam.

Harper said, "Jeannie! For God's sake, girl, what's wrong?"

Canton appeared, with another servant, in the dining-room door. Jeannie made an awful, blubbering noise, pointed a finger at him, and said in words barely discernible, "You . . . you did this . . . you changed the . . . plates . . ."

She spasmed and fell to the floor, jerking and twitching and vomiting, and then, with terrible swiftness, she stiffened, relaxed, and grew still. Her eyes, unseeing now, stared up at the ceiling.

Jeannie had been quite wrong. What she had imbibed was certainly no "pretty little poison."

Canton put his hand over his mouth, turned, and ran out of the house.

Harper, silent, knelt beside his daughter, looking into her face, his own face twisted in puzzlement. "She's dead?" he asked, looking up helplessly at Dex. "Jeannie's dead?"

Dex backed away, turned, and ran out of the house after Canton.

He found him in his little house, cringing in a corner, crying.

"Canton . . . Canton, listen to me. I need you to tell me something."

"She's dead, Dex! She's dead, she's dead, she's dead—"

"Canton, hush now. Hush. Listen to me, and answer me. After Jeannie was in the kitchen this evening, after you'd come up to see me and then gone back, did you change anything about the plates of food?"

"I . . . I . . . I can't remember what I did. She's dead, Dex!"

"You've got to remember, Canton. It's important."

"I . . . yes . . . I changed the pretty things on the plates. The pretty green things I put there . . . I decided they would look better different, and I changed them about. Miss Jeannie said to give her father the plate with the rose hip, so I moved the rose hip to the plate that looked the best. That's all I did. I swear, that's all."

"Oh, Lord. Oh, sweet Lord. She ate the very stuff she'd planned for him to get. . . ."

"What is it, Dex? What are you talking about?"

"Nothing. Never mind. Canton . . . there may be some trouble. Some questions. People might ask a lot of questions. . . . Sweet mama, I've got to think! Got to figure

189

out what to do now that things have gone so wrong. . . .''

Canton looked at him, confused and pleading, a manboy seeking help and explanation from the only person he'd known to trust through his years.

Dex stood, pacing about, thinking and trying not to panic. Everything was different now. The wealthy, free life he'd anticipated with Jeannie now was something that could never be. She'd set a snare for her father and fallen into it herself. Montgomery Harper was still alive, and Jeannie was dead. Dead! He couldn't quite fathom it.

There would be no inheritance. No freedom and wealth . . . and no escape from the probing of Montgomery Harper, who so obviously suspected Dex's embezzlements.

Good Lord, Dex thought, *they might try to put the blame for her death on me! It wouldn't be hard to dream up some motive for a husband to want to get rid of a wife. That kind of thing happens all the time. And even if they don't blame me, I still can't tell them the truth! I surely can't tell them it was all a mistake—that the poison should have gone to the old man!*

He turned to Canton. "Listen, boy, I want you to do something for me. I want you to say you don't know a thing about what happened."

"I *don't* know a thing."

"I know. I know. And that's good. Just tell them that. Don't talk about decorating the plates, or changing them about, or nothing. Just tell them that . . . I don't know. I can't think! This wasn't supposed to happen."

"Why did she die, Dex?"

"Because . . . I don't know. I don't know nothing. Neither do you. And I reckon that's all there is to it. You don't know nothing, I don't know nothing, and that's that." He paused. "Wait . . . the bottle! She was going to put the bottle in here to—" He abruptly stopped speaking, and began frantically searching around the little two-room house.

"Dex, what you doing?"

"I'm looking for something . . . a little bottle with a bit of powder in it."

"What bottle?"

"Never mind! Just help me look. And if you find it, give it to me . . . and then forget you ever saw it."

Canton stood and joined the search, looking just as frantically as Dex was, picking up, as usual, on his brother's emotional state.

It was Canton who found it. "Dex . . ." He turned, holding the bottle in his hand.

Dex lunged for it, identified it, and crammed it into his pocket. "Thank God!" he said. "Thank God!"

"What is that, Dex?"

"It's nothing, Canton. Nothing. You understand me? It's nothing you ever saw, ever touched, ever heard of. There was no bottle, no nothing. And you don't know a thing about how Jeannie died. You understand me?"

"Yes."

"There'll probably be questions. From Mr. Harper, from the law. Whatever they ask, you just tell them you don't know anything about what happened. You understand me? They ask you if Jeannie came to the kitchen today, you say you don't remember. They ask you anything about how the food was fixed today, you tell them there was nothing different, you don't know a thing. No matter who asks you, how hard they push, you tell them that. Understand?"

"Yes. Dex, am I in trouble? Did I make her die?"

"No, Canton. No. You didn't make her die. And I don't think you'll be in trouble, as long as you just do what I say, and tell them you don't know a thing." He reached over and patted Canton gently, like in the old days. Dex didn't consciously think about it, but he'd made a swift and major transition: The man who mere minutes before had been conspiring to let his helpless brother take the blame for murder was now frenetically concerned with protecting him—and protecting himself in the process.

"I'm scared, Dex."

"Just trust me, Canton . . . and whatever you do, don't remember a thing."

The door rattled, opened, and Montgomery Harper appeared. His leathery cattleman's face had an odd pallor; it looked like a mask pasted over his real face.

"She's dead," he said numbly. "My daughter is dead."

"I know," Dex said.

"Why did you run out of the house, Dex?"

"Because . . . of Canton. He was scared. I was . . . worried he'd be so upset he'd hurt himself."

"My daughter is dead."

"I know."

"Your wife, Dex. Your wife is dead, but you don't seem to care."

"I . . . I can't believe it, that's all. It doesn't seem real."

Harper's lip trembled. "You know why she died. I know that you do. Damn you, I know more about you than you think—about your thieving from the store and the saloon. *You* did it! *You* killed her! How did you do it, Dex? Poison? And why? *Why?*"

"You're talking out of your head, sir," Dex said. "I don't know what you're getting at, but I can tell you I had nothing to do with what happened. And I don't know what you're talking about, thieving from the store."

Harper lifted a trembling finger and aimed it at Dex's face. "You don't go anywhere tonight, Dex. I've sent for the sheriff, and there'll be questions. You don't set foot off this property until he gets here. You hear me?"

Without waiting for an answer, Harper wheeled and strode back toward the house.

Canton pulled his arms tight around himself and began a low, monotonous humming, something he'd done as a child when frightened, something Dex hadn't heard from him in a decade or more.

"Shut that up, Canton! Now!"

"We didn't do nothing, Dex! He's mad at us, and we didn't do nothing!"

"Canton, I was wrong before. We can't deny our way out of this. They won't believe us. We've got to get away from here. Now. In a minute or two it's going to strike Harper that we really might try to run, and he's going to put a gun on us and hold us for the sheriff. You got any food in here? Any money?"

"I got bread. And three dollars."

"Fetch it. I got a few dollars in my pocket, too. God, I wish I had my pistol with me! But I can't risk fetching it. Come on, Canton. We'll slip out that window, and keep this shed between us and the house until we're down at the creek. Then we'll go down a ways, and across, and over the hill to the road."

"We going to use our horses?"

"No time. We'll have to run on foot."

"But we didn't do nothing, Dex! Why are we having to run?"

"It's nothing you could understand. Come on. Let's go. There's no more time for talking."

The window wanted to stick, but together they were able to pull it up. Canton went out first, Dex following, and they ran across the meadow and for the creek, as hard as they could go.

Chapter Twenty

Four days later

Montgomery Harper eyed the big stranger closely, looking from the one good eye to the drooping one, and back again.

"So you want to find Dex Wilson for me, do you? Why?"

"Because of a lot of things, Mr. Harper. Because he owes me . . . and I owe him."

"Who are you?" The man had arrived at the Harper spread unheralded, a dirty trail bum with an ominous, dark manner about him, and a strange way of talking with only one side of his mouth moving.

"My name is Murchison. I been wanting to get my hands on Dex Otie for a good number of years now."

"Dex Otie? It's Dex *Wilson* I want. The bastard murdered my daughter, his own wife! And he's been embezzling money from me, and this after I'd made him part of my business, part of my family.''

''Dex Wilson *is* Dex Otie. Me and Dex go way back, we do.''

''You're sure they're one and the same?''

Devil Jack pulled a folded-up newspaper page from inside his vest. He unfolded it before Harper, revealing the big, lurid story that had run in the wake of Jeannie Harper Wilson's ugly death. It was a remarkably accurate and detailed story, as frontier newspaper stories went—Harper had made sure of it by cooperating with the reporter. He wanted Dex's identity known; he wanted the man caught and brought back.

''Mr. Harper, I've been looking for Dex Otie for months on end, and when I saw this story, I knew I'd found him. A long time ago, he took money that was mine, and vanished along with that fool brother of his. But in the meantime, he got me drawn into a gun battle up at Denver. . . . I came out alive, but hurt. I lost an eye, and the feeling and movement in half my face.

''I looked for Dex Otie for a long time after that, but there was no trail. I finally gave up on it, figuring he'd gotten away. But then I rode into Dodge City back toward the end of last year, right after a big fire that about wiped out half the town, and I seen a burned-out saloon wall with the names of Dex and Cant Wilson on it. It didn't take me long to find out that Dex and Cant Wilson were Dex and Canton Otie . . . and that they'd headed for East Texas. It was the first clue I'd had about them since Denver, and I came after them. Looking, asking questions. I was right up on finding Dex again when I saw this newspaper, and knew that the son of a bitch had gone and slipped past me again. But I commenced to thinking. I thought, *This Mr. Harper and me got something in common. He wants Dex as bad as I do.*

But my problem is I'm a poor man. I can't afford to hunt him forever. But you, sir, you ain't poor.''

"No. Far from it.''

"And you, sir, can afford to do what it takes, and pay what it takes, to find Dex Otie and bring him back.''

"I can. And I believe I see where you're going with this, Mr. Murchison. Which leaves me with one question. Why should I finance you, of all people, a stranger to me, to go after him?''

Murchison leaned slightly forward, his good eye glaring at Harper. "Because there ain't a living man under the sky what hates Dex Otie the way I do. He murdered my brother, sir. He took money that was rightfully mine, and left me a poor man. And he cost me this.'' He pointed at his dead eye, and his paralyzed lips. "I didn't give up searching for Dex Otie because I forgave him. Only because I had no trail to follow. Now I've got a trail. He can't have gone far, not with that brother in tow, not with no horse, no gun, no money but whatever he had in his pocket. I can find him. I *will* find him, whether you pay me for it or not. The only question for you, sir, is, when I find him, do you want your chance to get a piece of him for what he done to your daughter, or do you want me to have my satisfaction alone, and you to do without?''

Harper's eyes narrowed; he was thinking hard. "Mr. Murchison, sir, I have every reason to believe the forces of the law will find Dex Wilson—Dex *Otie,* if you're telling me right—entirely on their own. Why do I need to hire you?''

Murchison gave a chilling smile—half a smile, really, because of that half-paralyzed face. "Because when the law catches him, the law deals with him its way, not my way. Hell, he might find himself a sweet-talking lawyer and convince some jury he's innocent. 'Cause from what I read in this newspaper, there ain't a hell of a lot of evidence to convict him. The law catches him, he maybe snakes his way out of trouble. *I* catch him . . . there's no way out for him. I'll bring him back here, to you, alive, and we'll take our own kind of satisfaction for what he's done to us both. Personal. No trials, no lawyers, no soft-hearted juries. Just you, me . . . and him.''

Harper held silence, but his eyes were hungry. ''Why should I trust you? I don't even know you. What evidence can you give me that you'll do what you say?''

''Not a bit, sir. None but the evidence of your own gut when you look me in the eye. None but my firm promise to you that I want Dex Otie's hide more than any man alive, more even than you . . . and my promise that I'll bring him back to you. Look at me, Mr. Harper. What does your instinct tell you? Ain't I a man worth risking a few dollars on, just in case I *am* telling you the truth?''

Harper studied him. ''Yes. I believe you are.''

''So we're ready to deal, me and you?''

Harper paused only a moment. ''We're ready to deal.''

Dusk, two days later, twelve miles away, in an abandoned stable

Dex Otie sat glum, hungry, and very nearly hopeless, his eyes scanning again a copy of the same newspaper page that Murchison had spread before Harper.

He was trapped. No way out. In all these days he'd managed only to travel twelve miles, and not even to gain a weapon or half enough food. The rest of the time he'd been hidden out in places such as this, with Canton, both of them miserable and starving, both of them longing to flee, but unable to run because a man thoroughly described in every newspaper, running in company with an equally well-described half-wit, couldn't hope to evade detection.

If only I were alone, he thought, looking at Canton, who slept in a heap of ancient straw, curled into a fetal posture. *If only I didn't have Canton to slow me down and mark me, just like he was some cussed white elephant following me on a leash . . . I might be able to make it.*

The loyal and brotherly part of him that had managed to survive despite Jeannie hated to think this way, but he'd thought it many times now: *I should have left Canton behind, and run alone.*

He knew there would be no hope if he was caught. He had no good arguments to present on his own behalf, no good explanation about that poison . . . and Harper was rich, a man of influence. The verdict would be what Harper wanted it to be.

He gazed at his sleeping brother again, and thought, *I'm going to have to leave you, boy. I don't want to, but this time it's different than ever before. If I keep with you, I'll be caught. It's only a matter of time.*

The thought did not shock him; he'd thought it enough times lately that it now fit fairly comfortably into his mind. But still he hadn't been able to bring himself to act on it. To actually abandon Canton . . . could he really do it?

I can, he told himself urgently. *I can, because I have to. And why not? I was ready to go along with Jeannie and let him bear the blame for poisoning that food—so what's the difference now? God knows I've spent enough years taking care of him, sacrificing for him, risking my tail time and again, sharing food with him when there really wasn't enough for two. . . .*

It began to rain, lightly, but a peep through a knothole revealed clouds that were heavy and sodden; the truly hard rain would come soon and carry on through the night.

Rain that would wash away a man's tracks, and drive indoors those who might be on his trail.

He stared down at Canton, and his eyes filled with tears. The moment had come, but it wasn't easy. He ached to say good bye, and give Canton a long, brotherly hug . . . but it couldn't be. He could only leave if Canton was asleep.

Canton had been sleeping hard like this for the past two nights, and for part of the days as well. He seemed to be feeling poorly, feverish maybe. It was harder to leave him, knowing he was sick.

If I was noble and good, I'd stay with him no matter what. I'd take the consequences and never abandon him . . . if I was noble. If I was good.

Dex stood silently and choked back a sob. The rain began to fall harder, hammering the roof of the stable. He looked down at his sleeping brother.

"Good-bye, boy. I reckon you're own your own now."

And then he was gone.

He'd heard the sound of the train whistle several times during his residency in the stable, coming from the southwest. He headed that way through the driving storm. His feet sloshed in his shoes, his clothing clung to his skin, his hair and beard were pasted to his flesh. But he pushed on, heedless, pushed on, hard.

He saw the train by a flash of lightning, sitting at a whistle-stop. A couple of houses, a water tank, a shed and barn, a small train station. A few windows here and there were lighted; what humanity was about this place was safe indoors. He passed one of the houses; something moved in the window, and he ducked low. A face peered out, monstrously distorted by water running down the window, squinting into the storm. He ducked low until the face disappeared, then headed for the train.

Someone appeared on the train station porch, and he dodged for the nearest shed. The door was closed and padlocked, but someone had failed to close the lock and he slipped quickly inside, breathless and wondering if the man at the station had seen him.

He heard steps approaching. Hiding behind a stack of wooden crates, he sank low and tried to become the embodiment of silent nothingness.

The door opened; lantern light spilled inside. . . .

Dex sucked in his breath.

Whoever was at the door hefted the lantern around a bit but did not enter. The light receded, the door swung shut, and Dex waited for the inevitable clasping of the lock.

He didn't hear it. For whatever reason, the shed still was left unlocked. A faulty padlock, perhaps . . . it didn't matter why. What mattered was, he could still get out.

He left the shed, the storm still raging, and made for the parked train. He rolled into the first boxcar that had an unlatched door. It was full of crates and casks and lumber. He found a place to hide among the crates . . . and held back a yelp when another man rose up and looked at him curiously from behind another box.

"Howdy," the fellow said. Just a vagrant of the rails, friendly and probably harmless. "You're wet, my friend."

"Who are you?"

"Joe. That's all. Just plain Joe."

"You got any food on you, Joe?"

"A bit of dried beef."

"Well, sir, what might I offer you in return for a bit of it?"

"I'll share free. We who travel like this, we have to share with one another, eh?"

Dex nodded and smiled. "So we do."

The train rolled out when the storm abated, chugging through the night. Several miles down the track, a yelping, raggedly clad figure went hurtling out the partially open door of a boxcar and tumbled to the ground below.

The tramp named Joe stood, covered with mud, frowning bitterly after the departing train and the man who had cast him off—and that after taking almost every bit of his food! No true man of the rails that one was; true roaming men, the honorable kind, at least, cared for each other, didn't steal from each other—at least, not everything.

"On the run from the law, I betcha," Joe said aloud to the night. "By Gawd, I hope they catch him!"

He brushed as much mud as he could off his tattered garments and began striding back toward the train station, twisting his head only once to watch the train vanish into the darkness behind him.

The little boy named Hobie was black, impoverished, and very suspicious of most white men he met . . . but this one he wasn't sure how he felt about. He could tell at a glance that he was sick, curled up like he was in this old stable—now unused, nothing but an occasional play site for Hobie and his siblings, whenever they bothered to roam the mile required to get here from their little cabin house.

He crept forward and looked down at the curled-up fellow, thinking him asleep . . . but suddenly the face looked at his, eyes red, and the man gave a loud, sniffing sob.

Hobie jumped back and almost ran from the stable—but curiosity stopped him.

"Who you?" he asked.

The white man sat up. He was rough and weathered, but also looked sickly.

"He's gone. He's gone and left me."

Hobie stepped forward just a few inches. "Who?"

"My brother. He's gone. I was asleep and he was here, and when I woke up, he was gone."

Hobie could tell it now, no doubt about it: This fellow was dim-witted. He could see it in his eyes, hear it in his voice. He drew a little closer. "You sick, mister?"

"I'm sick. I been real sick. I'm hungry and alone. I'm scared."

Hobie had the odd sense of looking at a man much older than he, yet knowing that the fellow was really more of a boy than he was. "Can you walk?"

"I . . . I think I can."

"You on the run from something, mister?"

"There was trouble . . . back at Mr. Harper's."

"Harper!"

"Yes. Mr. Harper, he's mad. He thinks we done it, but we didn't! I swear we didn't!"

"You don't need to explain nothing to me, mister. If Montgomery Harper's your enemy, then you're my friend. You know what Harper done once? Had my daddy whipped. Said he'd stole a pig. It was a lie. He never stole nothing from Harper, but Harper had some of his men tie my daddy up and whip him with a knotted line. I hate him now. So does Daddy."

"I'm hungry."

Hobie smiled, a warm and open kind of smile. "We got food back home. Enough to share, and there's a place you could sleep. If you don't mind being with dark folk."

Canton Otie knew nothing of prejudice; it was one of the many realities of life that had escaped a man who

202

was perpetually and innately innocent, and always would be. "I can go with you?"

"Yep. If you want to. If you running from Harper, we'll keep you safe. I can promise you that, without even asking."

Canton stood, wobbly and weak, but stronger now because there was hope. He stepped forward, toward the black boy.

"My name's Hobie," he said. "What's yours?"

Canton almost answered, but he remembered how Dex had changed their names when he was trying to hide from Devil Jack. Maybe he should change his name again now. But his mind worked slowly, especially now that he was ill, and he couldn't think of one. So he finally admitted, "My name's Canton."

The boy grinned at him. "Howdy, Canton."

They set out together, side by side.

Chapter Twenty-one

The report came to the sheriff first, and from there to Montgomery Harper, who in turn wired it on—unbeknownst to the law—to Jack Murchison at the little community where Murchison had gone to investigate a prior report of a pair of men who might be the Otie brothers. A false lead, that one turned out to be, and as Murchison stood reading the translation of the coded message that had just clicked off the train station telegraph wire, he thought that this newest rumor, centering on another train station a few miles up the track from where Murchison happened to be just now, was even less likely to turn up Dex Otie.

Still, it was a lead, the only one he had, and so he mounted his horse and rode to the station in question, and upon his arrival promptly began inquiring among the people involved.

It appeared that a man had been seen at the station the night before, during the storm, running for the train and climbing into a boxcar. A Mexican woman inside the station had watched it all, but said nothing because there didn't happen to be anyone around at the moment who could understand her—not to mention that she had a certain sympathy for tramps, having a brother who sometimes followed that calling. Later, her English-speaking husband arrived, a man with less sympathy for vagabonds, and he, recalling the recent murder at the Harper ranch and knowing that the suspected culprits were still uncaught, had mentioned what his wife had seen.

Still, little was thought about this until shortly before dawn, when a tramp named Joe came walking back down the track, saying he'd been tossed from the boxcar by a man who'd taken his food and talked suspiciously. As Joe had thought it over during his trek back to the station, he'd come to think that maybe this fellow was one of the two being sought in that much-publicized poisoning death over at the Harper spread. His looks matched the description of one of them.

Quick telegraph work ensued. The lead had been transmitted on to the county sheriff, who immediately wired it to Harper via his private telegraph line, who in turn sent it on to Murchison. Now Murchison was here even before the more sluggardly representatives of the law showed up, enjoying the benefit of being the first questioner.

Joe was still about the train station, having been told to remain to answer questions, and Murchison sat down with him and began talking descriptions. The more this fellow talked, the more excited Murchison became.

It indeed sounded as if this man had had an encounter with Dex Otie. But if so, where was Canton?

An interesting question, but perhaps irrelevant, and certainly not one he intended to hang around trying to answer. Most likely he'd dumped Canton off somewhere, maybe even killed him, knowing that fleeing with a babble-spouter trailing along with him was like running with a grindstone tied to your foot.

"Where's that train now?" Murchison asked the station agent.

"Well, that's a funny thing," the fellow replied. "We just got in a wire—the dang thing's burned its bearings on two cars, and it's stalled down now on the track ten miles from the Blackwater station."

"You mean to tell me that train's just sitting on the track yonder?"

"That's right. The conductor sent a walker up on foot to Blackwater to wire in the news."

"How long until they'll be moving again?"

"Don't know."

Devil Jack turned and strode away, heading for his horse. He set out up the track, those at the station watching him go.

"Wonder what he's planning to do?" Joe asked.

"Don't know," the station agent replied, rather coolly. He had little use for tramps. "Going looking for that man he was asking about, I reckon."

"What kind of law was this fellow, anyhow?"

"I didn't ask."

"Funny how half his face was so stiff."

"You talk a lot for a tramp, partner. Why don't you go sit yourself down in the corner there and keep a lid on it awhile, huh?"

The agent watched the stranger disappear up the tracks, and wondered himself just what kind of law he was, and why he hadn't thought to ask about it. He sure wasn't a sheriff's deputy; the agent knew every one of them.

Maybe he shouldn't have shared information so freely with this man. Oh, well. Too late to worry about that now. He turned back to his desk and duties, and let it all slip out of his mind.

Devil Jack knew he'd stumbled upon a situation as soon as he was within spyglass range of the stranded freight train.

He descended from his saddle, no doubt a great relief to the exhausted horse. Dropping to his knee, he extended his pocket spyglass and peered through it. Slowly he smiled.

He'd found Dex Otie, all right. The man looked thin, worn, and wan, and shaky as a leaf, but it was Dex Otie, and he was standing beside one of the boxcars, a pistol in his hand, aimed at the assembled crew. One other man, Devil Jack noted, lay on the ground, unmoving, a few yards from Dex. Canton? It was hard to tell, but he didn't think so from what he could see. This man was much bigger than Canton.

Devil Jack lowered the spyglass, folded it, pocketed it. He wondered where Dex had gotten the pistol. The story going around was that the fugitives from the Harper spread weren't thought to be armed. He'd jumped the big fellow now on the ground, probably, and taken it.

Devil Jack mounted and made a wide circle, pushing the weary horse as hard as he could, and keeping the rise of the land between him and the train. Then, as he circled over, he did so in a way that blocked him from Dex's view, the train between Devil Jack and the apparent hostages.

He rode as close as he dared, then stopped his horse and dismounted. He tethered it to a little scrap of a tree and quickly checked his pistols. One he wore openly, tied into his holster, the other inside his coat, a hideout gun. Both were loaded.

He wasn't sure what Dex Otie, who obviously had

been discovered hiding in the train after the breakdown, had in mind for this little standoff of his. Maybe he had no plan at all and was merely acting out of desperation.

Either way, Devil Jack did have a plan, or part of one. Just behind the locomotive was a wood car, not quite full. Just behind the wood car was a boxcar with a still-smoking wheel—one of the cars afflicted with bearing trouble, obviously.

Devil Jack kept his eye on the wood car. If he was careful, he could climb into it without being seen by any of the group on the other side of the train. From there he could probably plunk a bullet right into Dex. Through the head? No. No. He wanted Dex to know who had found him and killed him. He wanted that much in memory of his brother Wade.

He reached the train and began climbing quietly into the wood car. For a moment, going over the side, he was exposed, but no one was looking his way. Dex still held their attention, just as he still held the pistol.

Devil Jack settled down on the heaped wood and listened.

Dex was talking. "I want these boxcars disengaged," he said. "Nothing but the locomotive and wood car—and you, conductor, I want you in that locomotive. You're going to ride me out of here."

Hell, Devil Jack thought. *He really is desperate! He thinks he can run away on a train?*

"Why should I help you?" the conductor asked, rather shakily.

The answer was a gunshot, followed instantly by a collective yell of alarm from the men. Devil Jack himself jerked in surprise, not having expected a shot.

"That's why," Dex said. "Next one's through your head." Devil Jack rose, peeped over the side, and saw Dex motioning a couple of the crewmen toward the train. "You two, get over there and uncouple those box-cars."

Jack ducked low again as the men approached. He listened to them working on the coupling, mere feet away from his hiding place. "There," one of them said. "It's done."

"Get back over here, and all you men lie down. All but you, conductor. And you, darky—you the fireman?"

"Yes, sir."

"You're coming with me, too. You try anything, and your conductor friend is dead, and you next. The rest of you, lie on the ground. Flat on your faces, and don't move for another hour."

Jack heard them getting on the ground, and footsteps heading toward the locomotive.

He considered. *I could rise up right now and shoot him dead. End this thing right here.*

But no. He wasn't quite ready for that. Let Dex have a bit more time. He was curious about where this little scheme was going to lead, and thinking how much fun it would be to let Dex think he'd really gotten away, only to find his old nemesis, probably long forgotten, suddenly alive in front of him, gun in hand.

The wood in the car was stacked in such a way to give Jack a recess in which he could ride hidden from the view of those in the locomotive. He nestled himself into the nook as Dex and his two prisoners climbed aboard the locomotive.

Dex was talking fast, barking orders, telling them to get the train in motion and to turn on all available speed.

Devil Jack grinned. This was going to be interesting. A train ride, followed by the death of Dex Otie. Appropriate, considering how all this had begun on a train. Jack wasn't a deep-thinking man, but he could appreciate a good piece of irony.

The train was soon in motion, smoke and sparks passing overhead above Jack in his hiding place. He peeped up around the stacked wood. Dex was in the locomotive, pistol against the conductor's neck. The fireman was busily feeding the boiler fire, and the train was moving faster by the moment.

"More speed!" Jack heard Dex order. "Faster!"

"You push it harder, mister, and this thing will jump the track when we hit the Blackwater bridge. That bridge is weak and has a sag—you got to hit it slow, really slow, or it's dangerous as rattlers!"

"Don't feed me lies, railroad man. You got every reason to want to slow me down. I want speed, all the speed you can get, and I don't want this train stopping at any stations. You go right on through, and take me as far as I can go."

"I'm telling you, mister, you hit the bridge at top speed, you'll be at the bottom of the gulch!"

"Shut up and go faster!"

And so they barreled on, the locomotive moving fast indeed, given that it had only the weight of one car behind it.

Devil Jack watched for his opportunity and rose silently. Drawing his pistol, he began to creep around and across the wood.

The fireman, sensing something, perhaps, turned and saw him. "What the—"

The train jolted over a rough section of track just as Dex turned in response to the fireman's exclamation. The entire locomotive lurched, jolted, and suddenly there was a blasting roar from inside.

Dex, jolted by the bump and surprised by the vision of Devil Jack Murchison arising like a demon from the wood in the car behind him, had accidentally fired off the unfamiliar and light-triggered pistol, which he had wrestled off the railroad crewman who had discovered him hiding in the boxcar.

The conductor groaned and leaned forward. Spurting blood sizzled against hot metal. The conductor slumped further and was dead, his body wedged against the throttle.

Dex hardly seemed to notice what had happened. "You!" he screamed at Devil Jack. *"You!"*

Devil Jack raised his pistol and fired at Dex's face. The motion of the train threw off his aim; the bullet struck metal and ricocheted, taking off the lobe of the fireman's left ear. He screeched, dropped to his knees.

Dex dropped, too, startled by Jack's gunshot. The train struck another rough section of track. Dex fell against the fireman, knocking him over, pushing against the door.

It wasn't thoroughly shut, and so pressed open under the fireman's weight. For a moment the terrified man leaned out into empty space, air rushing hard against his face. Then he fell.

He missed the racing wheels, but only by inches. Rolling down the side of the graded track, he came to his feet and half staggered, half ran, away from the track. The train quickly left him behind.

Dex rose, sticking his pistol out and firing blindly at Devil Jack.

It was a lucky shot. It caught Devil Jack in the right hand. He dropped his pistol with a screech.

Dex fired again, again, and yet again, but now the motion of the train hampered him, and he missed. When he pulled the trigger a fourth time, it clicked emptily.

The locomotive hurtled on, picking up speed on a slight downhill grade now, heading toward a spindly bridge over a deep gulch just now coming into view—though neither Devil Jack nor Dex saw it.

They saw only each other, and the long years of animosity on the one side, fear on the other, that stood between them.

Devil Jack came up and over the side of the wood car, leaping for the rear of the locomotive, reaching at the same time with his semiparalyzed left hand for the hideout gun beneath his coat.

He didn't quite make the leap. He caught himself, barely, and hung there between the locomotive and the wood car—and Dex's face peered over at him and broke into a cold, slow smile.

"So you're back from hell, are you, Devil?" Dex said. "Well, damn you, go back again! Go join your brother, Devil Jack!"

He hammered on Devil Jack's gripping fingers with the butt of the empty pistol. Hammered again and again, Devil Jack screeching and cursing, damning Dex in every way he could, and Dex meanwhile laughing like a man half mad.

Devil Jack screamed as his bloody fingers let go, and at the same moment somehow managed to bring up the hideout gun. He fired . . . and missed. And then he was under.

Dex laughed wildly. The train hurtled on. He'd done it! He'd escaped! And Devil Jack was gone, forever this time.

Back on the track, Devil Jack Murchison managed to sit up. He felt odd, painless, numb all over. Looking down, he saw and almost managed to actually accept that his legs were gone, sliced off neatly by the racing wheels of the wood car. Blood spread around him, far too rapidly. He watched it with a strange sense of dispassion.

Then he lifted his head, just as the hurtling train hit the bridge at top speed. He watched, his eyes widening, his lips spreading into a trembling grin.

"Gotcha, Dex!" he said. "Gotcha . . ."

He still had the smile on his face when he died.

The locomotive careened into the air like an arrow fired from a weak bow, curving out and down in a graceful and strangely beautiful arc. Curling smoke from the locomotive stack traced a crescenting course toward the gorge bottom fifty feet below.

Dex Otie screamed all the way to the bottom, high and childishly and so loud that he ruptured his own vocal cords just before it all ended.

The locomotive struck bottom in a burst of fire and an explosion of shredding metal. Dex Otie was only vaguely conscious of his body being ripped asunder, and of flame enwrapping him.

The locomotive had caught some of the bridge's key supports on its way down, and now the bridge collapsed, falling in atop the burning engine, crushing it down, giving it new fuel to burn.

And burn it did, for the longest time, black smoke rising from the bottom of the gulch, carrying the smell of charred metal, burning wood, and searing flesh.

Chapter Twenty-two

Three weeks later

Their skin was black, all but one of them. The Arkansas-bound family sat huddled in their battered old wagon. Hobie sat beside his father and mother. In the back, among the jumble of furniture and other goods, sat brothers and sisters, and the strange, simple-minded white man who had only weeks before become one of the family. Not by plan or design. Hobie had brought him home, that was all, and he had somehow managed to find a place.

His name was Canton, and they liked him, were glad he was with them.

The wagon sat far too close to the edge of the Blackwater gulch, and those on it peered over the edge, craning their necks to see the activity below—railroad crews, still cleaning up the incredible wreckage of a bridge, a locomotive, and a burned-up railroad wood car.

"They say there was a man in the locomotive. Or a little bit of something that was a man once, leastways," the eldest of the family said.

"I wonder who he was," Hobie said.

"Don't know. Then again, I ain't asked. None of my business. Whoever he was, wouldn't want to be him."

"There was another man they found, too," one of the children said. "On the tracks with his legs cut off."

"Better him than me, that's all I can say," the father replied. "Well, folks, we got us a long piece to travel, and I say let's get moving. Arkansas is waiting."

They rode on. Canton looked back, staring across the Texas landscape.

One of the children, a girl of about ten, looked up at him. "You thinking 'bout that brother who left you behind?"

"Yes."

"It was bad of him to leave you. Don't think 'bout him no more."

"I wonder if ever I'll see him again," Canton said. "He was good to me, most the time. I miss him."

"Maybe he'll find you someday."

"Maybe he will. Dex will do that, if he can."

"And if he don't, you still got us," she said.

Canton smiled at her. "I like you," he said. "I like all of you."

Her smile in return was bright. "I like you, too, Canton."

The wagon rolled on, Arkansas-bound.

THE LAST WARPATH

"The most critically acclaimed Western writer of this or any other time!"
—Loren D. Estleman

The battle between the U.S. Cavalry and the wild-riding Cheyenne, lords of the North Prairie, rages across the Western plains for forty years. The white man demands peace or total war, and the Cheyenne will not pay the price of peace. Great leaders like Little Wolf and Dull Knife know their people are meant to range with the eagle and the wolf. The mighty Cheyenne will fight to be free until the last warrior has gone forever upon the last warpath.

FIVE-TIME WINNER OF THE
GOLDEN SPUR AWARD

WILL HENRY

WHO RIDES WITH WYATT

"Some of the best writing the American West can claim!"
—Brian Garfield, Bestselling Author of Death Wish

They call Tombstone the Sodom in the Sagebrush. It is a town of smoking guns and raw guts, stage stick-ups and cattle runoffs, blazing shotguns and men bleeding in the streets. Then Wyatt Earp comes to town and pins on a badge. Before he leaves Tombstone, the lean, tall man with ice-blue eyes, a thick mustache and a long-barreled Colt becomes a legend, the greatest gunfighter of all time.

*BY THE FIVE-TIME WINNER OF THE
GOLDEN SPUR AWARD*

___4292-4 $3.99 US/$4.99 CAN

WILL HENRY
JOURNEY TO SHILOH

While the bloody War Between the States is ripping the country apart, Buck Burnet can only pray that the fighting will last until he can earn himself a share of the glory. Together with a ragtag band of youths who call themselves the Concho County Comanches, Buck sets out to drive the damn Yankees out of his beloved Confederacy. But the trail from the plains of Texas to the killing fields of Tennessee is full of danger. Buck and his comrades must fight the uncontrollable fury of nature and the unfathomable treachery of men. And when the brave Rebels finally meet up with their army, they must face the greatest challenge of all: a merciless battle against the forces of Grant and Sherman that will truly prove that war is hell.

_4203-7 $4.50 US/$5.50 CAN

Dorchester Publishing Co., Inc.
P.O. Box 6640
Wayne, PA 19087-8640

Please add $1.75 for shipping and handling for the first book and $.50 for each book thereafter. NY, NYC, and PA residents, please add appropriate sales tax. No cash, stamps, or C.O.D.s. All orders shipped within 6 weeks via postal service book rate. Canadian orders require $2.00 extra postage and must be paid in U.S. dollars through a U.S. banking facility.

Name_____
Address_____
City_____State_____Zip_____
I have enclosed $_____ in payment for the checked book(s).
Payment <u>must</u> accompany all orders. ☐ Please send a free catalog.

"Max Brand is a topnotcher!"
—*The New York Times*

King Charlie. Lord of sagebrush and saddle leather, leader of outlaws and renegades, Charlie rules the wild territory with a fist of iron. But the times are changing, the land is being tamed, and men like Charlie are quickly fading into legend. Before his empire disappears into the sunset, Charlie swears he'll pass his legacy on to only one man: the ornery cuss who can claim it with bullets—or blood.

_4182-0 $4.50 US/$5.50 CAN

Red Devil of the Range. Only two things in this world are worth a damn to young Ever Winton—his Uncle Clay and the mighty Red Pacer, the wildest, most untamable piece of horseflesh in the West. Then in one black hour they are both gone—and Ever knows he has to get them both back. He'll do whatever it takes, even if it costs his life—or somebody else's.

_4122-7 $4.50 US/$5.50 CAN

THE WORLD'S MOST
CELEBRATED WESTERN WRITER!

Donnegan. He comes from out of the sunset—a stranger with a sizzling six-gun. Legend says that he is Donnegan. And every boomtown rat knows he has a bullet ready for any fool who crosses him. But even though the Old West has fools enough to keep Donnegan's pistols blazing, the sure shot has his sights set on a certain sidewinder, and blasting the deadly gunman to hell will be the sweetest revenge any hombre ever tasted.

_4086-7 $4.50 US/$5.50 CAN

The White Wolf. Tucker Crosden breeds his dogs to be champions. Yet even by the frontiersman's brutal standards, the bull terrier called White Wolf is special. And Crosden has great plans for the dog until it gives in to the blood-hungry laws of nature. But he never reckons that his prize animal will run at the head of a wolf pack, or that a trick of fate will throw them together in a desperate battle to the death.

_3870-6 $4.50 US/$5.50 CAN

Dorchester Publishing Co., Inc.
P.O. Box 6640
Wayne, PA 19087-8640

Please add $1.75 for shipping and handling for the first book and $.50 for each book thereafter. NY, NYC, and PA residents, please add appropriate sales tax. No cash, stamps, or C.O.D.s. All orders shipped within 6 weeks via postal service book rate. Canadian orders require $2.00 extra postage and must be paid in U.S. dollars through a U.S. banking facility.

Name_____
Address_____
City_____ State _____ Zip_____
I have enclosed $_____ in payment for the checked book(s).
Payment <u>must</u> accompany all orders. ☐ Please send a free catalog.

RIP-ROARIN' ACTION AND ADVENTURE BY THE WORLD'S MOST CELEBRATED WESTERN WRITER!

GUN GENTLEMEN

MAX BRAND

Renowned throughout the Old West, Lucky Bill has the reputation of a natural battler. Yet he is no remorseless killer. He only outdraws any gunslinger crazy enough to pull a six-shooter first. Then Bill finds himself on the wrong side of the law, and plenty of greenhorns and gringos set their sights on collecting the price on his head. But Bill refuses to turn tail and run. He swears he'll clear his name and live a free man before he'll be hunted down and trapped like an animal.

_3937-0 $4.50 US/$5.50 CAN